# Fables

# and Fabrications

From the arctic wastes of Norway to a fun-laden evening at the fair, Jan Edwards leads us through a world where nothing is as it seems. Shape changers and ancient spirits roam, and cats play their inscrutable parts in stories that unsettle and disturb the reader's perceptions. Fourteen tales of mystery, mirth and the macabre. Chosen from her back catalogue of horror and dark fantasy, these stories, leavened with a sprinkle of verse, have been collected for the first time in this volume.

On 'Drawing Down the Moon': 'Jan Edwards has yet to let me down' – Dave Brzeski, British Fantasy Society

On 'Midnight Twilight': 'A really good story made brilliant by the final reveal' – Jim Macleod, Ginger Nuts of Horror

On 'A Taste of Culture': 'One of the stories that makes [*The Mammoth Book of Dracula*] a keeper' – N. Light, Amazon.com

To Peter and Misha


And to all of the Alchemists, Renegades
and Weirdos:

they know who they are!

First edition

ISBN 978-0-9930008-4-3

Penkhull Slim
Published by The Penkhull Press
Staffordshire

# Contents

# Acknowledgments

'A Taste of Culture', *Mammoth Book of Dracula*, Robinson Press 1997

'City Canal', *Whispers in the Wind*, Anchor Press 2001

'Corinna's Reply', *Salvo 7*, CHWG 2003

'Damnation Seize My Soul', *Dark Currents*, Newcon Press 2012

'Drawing Down the Moon', *Grimorium Verum,* Western Legends 2015

'Gallery Green', *Terror Scribes*, Dog Horn Publishing 2012

'Green Tea', *Salvo 8*, CHWG 2015

'Grey Magic for Cat Lovers', *New Horizons,* BFS 2011

'Jack Jumps Out of the Box', *Father Grimm's Story Book*, Wicked East 2012

'Mayday Comes Askew', *Tales from the Greenmantle* 2011

'Midnight Twilight', *Alt-Zombie*, Hersham Horror 2012

'Old Hat', *Salvo 6* CHWG, 2000

'Pet Therapy', *Demonologia Biblica,* Western Legends 2013

'Princess Born', *Grimm and Grimmer 1*, Fringe Works 2013

'The Abused and Him', *Visionary Tongue 6.* Visionary Tongue, 1996

'Thirteenth Day', *Estronomicon*, Screaming Dreams 2011

'Time's Excuses', *Through Clouds of Despair.* Triumph House 2001

'Wind Blows the Oaks' *Salvo 7*, CHWG 2003

'Winter Eve', *Ethereal Tales 9*, Ethereal Tales 2010

'You And Me Pop', public performance at *Dysprosium (Eastercon)*, 2015

All of the Haikus are original to this volume

# Drawing Down the Moon

CINTHIA SWEPT HAIR from her damp forehead and adjusted the kidskin eye patch. In the heat of the *Athena Taverna*'s kitchen sweat always gathered beneath the leather pad, sticky and cloying like the blood that had fallen at the eyeball's loss.

She put the memory aside and slid two slightly charred sausages onto an already loaded plate. She never understood this English obsession with breakfast, but it was her bread and butter; a word play that amused her as she cut two slices of rubbery white-bread toast into precision triangles and arranged them beside the oily fry-up. Her customers seldom noticed such finesse but it was attention to detail that got her through the steady stream of days peopled by a steady stream of workers. They tramped through the *Athena* from seven every morning till six at night; all drawn to her greasy-spoon cafe like snails to discarded lettuce. That day, in the teeth of a force nine, the stream was slowed to a bare trickle.

The radio churned out its diet of pop, a driving drumbeat. *Bang Bang* *Glad all over*. Cin tapped her fingers on the double-beat. She liked the song well enough but tonight such irrepressible cheeriness was more than she could take. She reached out and switched it off.

She took the loaded plate through the swing door to

dump it in front of a grubby tanker driver and walked on to the front window without a word to stare into darkness. Antony was late, as he often had been in recent weeks. *Sheltering somewhere warm*, she told herself. The seafront on Canvey Island was not a good spot to linger in January. The English told her how they imagined Greece was hot and dry twelve months of the year, but it could be cold and wet in Larissa, perhaps not like this, but cold enough. Twenty years in that place, when she had lived a hundred-score times that, was little more than a blink, yet still she missed home.

Cin glanced back at her lone customer with his head down at the trough and unaware. Perhaps she would risk it. She signed a row of arcane symbols into the window's moistness with her finger nail, then, and, just as quickly, eradicated them with a huff of breath.

Elementals resisted her will and flung a last whiplash of sandy water against the outer side, before they died away. Cin watched the shadows beyond the street lights for a while longer, and had barely registered the rise of voices when the half-eaten meal slammed into the glass beside her.

'What's your bloody game? I only just started that.'

'Go buy yourself another.' A muscle-man was stuffing ten-bob notes into the hands of her diner. 'Mrs Kolovos's got an urgent appointment.' He looked up at Cin, and grinned. 'With Mr Kolovos.'

'Yeah, but...'

'Private business. On your way, son.'

The lorry driver stared at Cin, spread hands closing into fists.

She shook her head, pulling her overall around her

like a security blanket. Sweet to offer but there was no need for anyone else to be damaged on her behalf. 'Go,' she said. 'Please.' The man hesitated and she patted his arm. Her ex-husband was not someone she wished on anyone. She had lived through many men over her long existence, but Jeno, her last, was her least palatable. Violence she was accustomed to: Jeno's psychosis was manifestly different.

She watched her solitary customer trail out into the rain and knew he would never be back. She shot the door-bolts behind him, leaning against the wood frame as if to gather strength from it. 'So where is he?' she asked, without turning round. 'Mr Kolovos is here?'

'The car's waitin',' was the heavy's only answer. He swept his hand toward the rear exit. 'Mrs Kolovos?'

'And if I say no?'

The man smirked and handed her a slip of paper.

Cin unfolded it and read, *If you wish to speak with our son bring all that you need.* A single sentence without salutation or signing off. None were needed.

It was an effort of will but she maintained an outer calm. Her boy. That monster had her boy. Antony was twenty years old, almost of age, but still her baby boy.

She breathed deep, nostrils widening as she fought down all hint of emotion and refolded the paper; sharpening the creases between thumb and forefinger as she considered her options. They were, lamentably, in the singular but she needed that brief space to centre her mind and assert self-control. 'Very well.' She brushed past him, chin held high. Bandying words with Jeno's lackeys would not serve her well.

In the tiny back office she took her time removing her

overall and netted snood; running her fingers through her long hair; dabbing colour to her lips. Brushing specks from her sweater and smoothing her pencil skirt, and wishing she was not stinking of greasy English breakfasts; taking her time because all the while she was here, then Antony was safe at least until she faced Jeno down. Finally she bent to the squat safe tucked beneath the desk and removed a canvas bag.

It was all that she needed; all that *he* needed.

*

The Humber finally drew up in a private road, twenty minutes and a world away from her own seafront pitch. This was no cookie-cutter housing. This was designer-built Modernism. *Ultra*-modern in glass and white concrete, long and low with a wide gravel drive. It screamed money but she doubted Jeno lived there. Jeno was a Knightsbridge kind of man. Even the best that Basildon could offer would be slumming it in his eyes.

The inside was a sparkling of white. White walls, pale marbled mosaic floors, white and grey furnishings. *Classic*, she thought. *No. Clinical. Not a thing out of place. Not a hint of colour.* It made her wince.

At the chrome cocktail bar set cater-corner on the farthest side of the room were three men; their backs firmly turned to her. As she was hustled in the eldest of them set his glass down, crossed the echoing expanse of mosaic, and continued around her, inspecting Cin minutely, like a farmer at a livestock auction. 'You've been elusive, Cinthia, my dearest,' he murmured.

*That*, she thought, *sums him up. He sees commodities. Never people.* 'I have been here all the time,' she replied. 'I have not hidden who I am.'

'But the *what*, my dear. Oh, *what* you have become makes all the difference after the Sisters. Such a come down.'

She pulled away from fingertips that trailed over her left cheek, just a fraction below the kidskin patch. She projected control, though every other part of her wanted to curl into a quivering ball and wait for the world's end. 'Why am I here?' She set her voice lower, quieter, where the cracks could not show. 'What are you doing with my son?'

'So hostile. No hello after all these years, my sweet?'

His second touch caught her unaware, tripping revulsion and anger in equal measure. She grasped his wrist. 'Never *your* sweet.' She took a deep breath, seeking control. 'Why, Jeno? We do you no harm. What do you want?'

'A favour. Or should that be a boon? An indulgence? I believe those were the terms your sisterhood required.'

'That was a time of war,' she replied. 'That was our past.'

'I think you could be persuaded.' He looked toward the bar. 'Antony is quite the young man now. Yet still your child, yes?'

She had not looked at her boy, hoping in some vague way that in not acknowledging him he would not be a part of this. He was tall and fair; the very image of his father, which had always pained her. He was so wholly Jeno's son, without a hint of her Greek curls and olive skin. When he lifted that blond head and slid from the bar stool to face her it was not his eyes she saw. Her gaze locked onto the rope linking his skinny wrists. It broke her heart. Her boy a captive, though it renewed her conviction that he was not a willing part of Jeno's charade. She went to move forward, to go to him, but Jeno's fingers clamped around her arm, digging white grooves into her skin.

'Your child also,' she said. 'Yet you would use him?'

'If you do as we ask we won't have to.'

She laughed, sharp and guttural, and wondered why he spoke of himself in third person. Nothing they had done together had ever warranted a 'we'. 'There is a traditional price. You know it,' she said.

'A child or an eye. I'm aware of that.' He touched her face again and she tensed, despite herself. His finger nail clicked along the edge of the eye piece, lifting it a fraction and letting it snap back against her socket.

Leaning forward she whispered, 'Bastard.'

'Is that the best you have?' he muttered.

She stopped breathing not wanting to draw in his breath; that familiar scent of coffee, cigarettes and mint. She turned her head away. 'Why?' she said again. 'Why do you want me blind?'

'Oh, good heavens woman. Why must you make this about you? I need a dead man's words and there is only one way to hear them.' He snorted. 'You could choose for yourself. You want to see all this? Think about what you had.' He stroked her hair, smoothing the curls that spiralled tighter in damp air and he laughed. 'No. *You* will be the noble woman once more.' He chuckled. 'Don't worry my little witch. You'll be well compensated. And you can go home at last. No more hiding.'

'My home is here. What good would returning to Thessaly do for me when I would not see it?'

'You'd have your son to tell you all about it,' he replied. 'Or you could see your homeland if you wished. If you take the second choice then *he* would not.'

'And if I refuse either path?'

'Then neither of you will ever see anything, ever. Or hear it. Or touch it. Or smell it.'

'And you would still not have your information.'

'True.' He leaned in and licked her ear. Cin managed not to shudder. 'I would not have my answers but it would tie loose ends very neatly.'

His face was just inches from hers. That odour once again. The aromas of tobacco and mint were inexorably linked with the mountain retreat in '44, where her sisterhood sheltered the Resistance. She had lost an eye there to this monster and fled the temple. Twenty long years of exile to keep her boy. She had brokered so many other mortal conceptions over the centuries, but none of those had mattered. Only her boy. The one life that she had desired to grow. If she agreed to Jeno's terms her boy would be safe. Only one last bargain to be endured and he could never ask again, because she would have no more to give. She closed her one eye. Now was not the time to sink into weakness. 'What is it you wish me to do?'

'The only thing I have ever asked of you.' He waved a hand. 'Draw down the moon, my sweetness.'

*

Double doors were flung opened into a wide loggia. If the sitting room had been minimalist then this was Spartan. Sliding glass doors took up three sides, with voile drapes drawn back into loose columns. The floor was the same mosaic of white and grey marble. The furnishings limited to a large fountain with a central column trickling water from triple spouts, and to one side of that a marble table; on which the obvious outline of a body lurked beneath a pale sheet.

It stank.

It reeked of that old familiar charnality and she lifted her nose toward it from instinct, like a hungry she-bear scenting tethered sheep. She knew that smell. She looked to the darkness beyond, at winter lashing glass walls and allowed herself one sigh; and then moved forward to flip the cloth back.

Her subject had been youngish in life, possibly handsome in a homely fashion. She did not need to touch him to ascertain he was dead. If the cloying stench had not been proof enough his unnatural colouring told her that blood has ceased flowing a week ago, and more.

'You want me to raise this?' she said. 'This is not a corpse, Jeno. This is dangerously close to being a puddle.'

'He passed on a few days ago, I agree. But we had to wait on the moon ripening.'

She did not correct him. The moon could be called a week before or after full but he did not need encouragement. 'Too long,' she said. 'His soul will have moved on.'

'We have done what we can to tether him. Salt, Skullcap, Red Pepper and Sulphur.'

She shrugged. 'It may work. Or he may be too far removed from this plane to remember. I can guarantee nothing. Who was he?'

'A no-one.'

'A no-one with a very expensive house.'

'A no-one who kept accounts using a somewhat imaginative method. I don't like that in my staff.'

'I remember.' She pursed her lips, gazing intently at the waxen face; at the dark bruising around his eyes and jaw; at cuts over his left eye and along his lips and at wrists banded raw from brutal restraint. This man had taken a systematic beating before he had slipped down to the banks of the Styx. She *was* glad it was winter, when flies were scarcer, or this man would be devolving into a sack of liquefying decay, awash with maggots and mould. It was not her concern, she did not know him; yet she felt kindred with any creature guilty of little more than gulling Jeno Kovolos.

'What must I ask?'

'Ask him for the numbers.'

'An accountant must know many numbers.' She tried to be nonchalant; keep her excitement on the ebb. If Jeno wanted this information and was prepared to go to these lengths for it then it must be valuable. 'If I am to ask the questions I need that much.'

'If he rises, then you will be told.'

She nodded. 'I must prepare.' She took a leather roll from her canvas bag and set it down on the edge of the table. Her hand lingered there, caressing the aged hide, fingers rippling across its embossed patterning. Its touch was exhilarating and she tensed; determined that her audience would not recognise her excitement.

Jeno's handsome face was creased into vulpine lines of stealthy anticipation, and she would wipe it away if she could. If it was the last thing she saw then it would be worth the sacrifice. Were it not for Antony.

*An eye or a child*; that was the traditional price paid for what he asked. 'One more thing,' she said. 'The body must be burned after the ritual. Or he will be trapped here, and he will follow you to your end.'

'That much I remember.' Jeno was less fox now and more wolf. 'This place,' he gestured around them. 'This house? A fitting pyre, since it was bought from my money.'

'So be it,' she agreed. 'Wash him. Infusions of rosemary and sage to purify. I am sure his kitchen can oblige.'

'You were to bring it all with you. I was quite clear.'

She raised her chin, looking down on him from a metaphoric height. 'I have all that I need. You bound him? You cleanse him.'

'I've missed our sweet nothings, Cinthia. Always an emotional feast.'

She held her ground. 'I say what needs to be said.'

Jeno sighed and snapped his fingers to his aide. 'You heard the lady. Wash our friend here.'

The verbal sparring rattled Cin more than she had thought possible. *I'm out of practice, or just getting old.* She went to the glass wall and flung open two of the sliding sections. Wind and rain surged over, around and past her angular form.

She breathed in the ozone-laden moisture and remembered how she had stood on the hillside within the temple grounds on many such nights as for old enmity he held for her sisterhood.

Wilder elements always focussed her psyche. This rite was something she had not anticipated acting out ever again, yet it was always there; waiting in the shadows for her to reach out and pluck it into the semi-light.

Kicking off her shoes she shed her coat, letting it slip free of her fingers. She unzipped her skirt and allowed it to drop around her ankles. *I who have nothing*, she crooned into the room's silence, and smiled. In the old days men were crazed by the notion of spying on her order. In the old days the Sisters would have crazed any man known to risk that spying. She unbuttoned her blouse as she hummed the recent ballad, swaying her hips, taking her time, taunting. Any added emotion her audience brought to the rite was to be welcomed.

She stood tall in nothing but black chemise and composure. Long ago she would have been naked but temperature ruled against it. They would have their floor show soon enough. Let them leer, allow them anticipation.

Her lips moved, like a slow reader, not singing now but chanting. To herself first, and then more loudly as her conscious merged with the echoes of beyond. She called on the Keres, daughters of Nyx, on Mnemosyne and Bia and on Lethe, but most of all she called to Styx and to Hecate. She slipped into the ritual as a ripe and luscious strawberry slides into the rich, sweet, darkness of chocolate. She became the rite, the vessel, through which the tendrils wafting off the Veil strayed into this world.

Energised by her actions she moved to the fountain; stretching her arms toward the spigots, whirling three times in a twisted, fluid dance; aping the very water. She swayed beneath the liquid, allowing it to cascade around her neck and shoulders before throwing her head back to loose a wild ululation. She called once again upon Hecate and Styx to allow the soul departed a brief return.

From beyond the clouds she felt the pull of the moon. It called her and she called back, repeating her watery dance twice more. Then she dropped to the hard, cool floor; prostrating herself before her elementals, with arms outstretched.

Wind rattled the glass, reaching into the room and splaying the fountain's water flow in its passing, rippling the voile curtains into horizontal.

Whilst this Thessalian woman worked her dark acts; diving into the world of shades and emerging with an act of full blown necromancy, just two pairs of eyes watched her, in thrall as the bodyguards, having washed the corpse had withdrawn; apparently not to be privy to any information the deceased might have.

Cin saw Jeno.

Cin saw her boy.

Their heads were almost touching. She saw them both look at her, and whisper to each other.

Betrayal? Was he also a man? Mid-rite she could not permit her own wants to intrude. She could not, would not, see her boy intimate with the man who killed so lightly.

The storm cut off as though a switch had been flicked. Where there had been only cloud, a harsh moonlight slotted across the untidy shagginess of blasted borders and winter lawns, glinting off the door panes and onto the woman who waited for its touch.

Cinthia swept off her eye patch to expose a puckered depression. Deliberately, elegantly, she came up to full height with arms up and rigid fingers splayed wide. She flexed each digit, clawing at the shaft of light, emitting a litany of noise from deep in her throat.

Listeners could not discern words in either Greek or English, but there was an unmistakable cadence placed on the edges of those notes that shredded nerves as surely as cat-claws down velvet curtains.

The moon's colour changed, starting on one side and creeping across its face, growing deeper and larger than its silvery persona. It had taken on a reddish hue, hanging low, resting on the jagged horizon of surrounding rooftops; a fecund and brooding night bird waiting to drop on its prey.

Cin's mutilated eye-socket echoed the swollen and bloody lunar form. Her one good eye was fully dilated; the iris pushed back to form a thin rind around deep blackness. Both sockets leaked dark, viscous blood, bisecting her cheeks and accentuating her jawline.

She strode to the head of the corpse and pulled the lace securing her rolled packet of ceremonials and stretched it out to reveal the tools of her trade; mostly herbs and unguents since her powers had always lain in her memory and her tongue. She withdrew a thick short wand of olive wood tipped with a polished smoked-quartz point that was bound in place by beaten copper. She took a small phial and opened it, spilling a little of its oily contents onto the wand, slowly running her fingers back and fore along the shaft, lost in the moment.

It had been so long since she had felt the sting of belladonna, henbane and mandrake; those herbs that set her racing across land and sky, leaving all that was earthbound in her wake. She rubbed more of the oil on the inside of each wrist and on her neck and on her groin; where her blood pulsed at its strongest. A final dab was placed on the centre of her forehead and her senses jolted, her night sight coming into sharp relief.

Cin breathed deep; calling loudly for the spirits to hear her, visualising her feet rooting into the stone beneath her, anchoring her to the earth against the effects of flying oils that would have her soaring up to greet the red moon.

Dipping her finger tips into the blood still coursing down her face, she anointed the dead man's eyes and lips.

She tipped her head back and screamed words in ancient tongues, but transmogrified into syllables that all could understand. 'Hecate, dark queen, Hecate, holy mother, lend this body its departed spirit I beg of you. Hecate, dark queen, Hecate, holy mother, lend this body its departed spirit.' repeated over and over in urgent supplication.

Cin reached into the kit for phials of wormwood and vervain and grave dust. She sprinkled a little of each into the dead man's open mouth. Then, gripping his head with steely fingers, she spat her dark fluids onto eyes and maw.

The corpse stirred and emitted a low moan. He sat up and stared at his nakedness. The stench of putrefaction wafted from his parted lips. Clearing his throat to speak, a shower of maggots flew out in front of him to patter softly across skin, table and floor. He stared at them for a moment, watching them writhe and flip in blind search of the darkness they had just vacated.

'Welcome – friend.' Cin leaned in to speak quietly into his confusion.

'Hello. I think ... I...' he jerked his attention away from the wriggling larvae and looked her in the eyes. 'I know your voice. You were calling... But I don't know you.' He swayed, his head drooping.'

Cin gripped his chin firmly and forced him to look at her. 'Welcome.' She wanted to look at Jeno yet knew she could not afford to lose contact with the returned soul at this pivotal stage. 'Welcome friend. We thank you for making the long journey. There are those here with questions that only you may answer.'

'Who? I don't know.'

He sagged, and as his face slipped from her blood and oil slicked hand it shimmered. Cin frowned, seeing his death mask already beginning to reassert possession and knowing he would be gone in a minute or two.

'I need his name.' Cin glared at Jeno. 'He was away too long. He's barely sentient. Don't play games, Jeno Kolovos. I need his name. Now!'

'Douglas,' Jeno replied.

'Douglas what?'

'For your own sake, my pet, ask only what you need.'

The corpse moaned; a mere whispering of escaped air. Cin glanced up at a fresh disturbance to her delicate sacrament. A scent distracted her. Blue-grey tobacco smoke polluting her ritual with its sharpness. She snapped around to see who would be so arrogant to break into her communing.

Antony took another furtive drag from the cigarette in his right hand and smiled at her; all insolence that was devoid of humour. It took a moment in her miasmic state to take in the facts. He was alone, unbound, unconcerned.

*Unbound.*

Her boy.

Douglas coughed, spraying out another small scatter of maggots. His life-force was soaking away. Too long dead for her ritual to take. And even if he were not the window was small without the bolstering energy of her sisterhood to sustain her.

'Douglas,' she called. 'Doug? Dougie?'

'What? No. Let me go.'

'Numbers, Dougie. You can tell me, can't you? And then you can go back. The numbers, Dougie.'

'Numbers. I like numbers. I think…' His pale, milky eyes rolled up in his head.

'Douglas!'

He was fading back to Hades from whence he had come from whence he belonged, taking Jeno's numbers with him. Cin looked around her, wondering what she could do. There was so much to lose; her own life being chief amongst them. Drastic measures were required.

'Jeno? You said you'd tell me when I needed to know. Well, I need to know. He's going, and no sacrifices will get him back a second time.'

Jeno hesitated, looking toward their son. A silent conversing of nods passed between them and Cinthia felt herself rising up on her emotions. What a fool. What a one-eyed and wholly blind fool.

*His* boy. No longer *hers*. He was his *father's* son. *His* boy.

The bargain shifted.

'Accounts,' Jeno said. 'The Swiss numbers.'

'That is all?' She asked.

Jeno inclined his head.

Douglas was losing strength by the second and his neck flopped in her grasp. 'Pray your games have not delayed this too long, Jeno.' She slapped Douglas hard and then cradled him against her chest. She sensed he was not yet gone. 'Swiss bank accounts,' she cooed in his ear. 'Tell me, Douglas. Then you may rest.'

The eyelids flickered for a moment.

She reached for her ritual tools and laid the crystal end of her wand against his forehead. 'Hecate, Goddess of the underworlds, lend him strength. Allow this soul to speak the words. Hecate hear me, hear your humble daughter. Take my sacrifice given with free will.'

She touched the crystal to her good eye.

There was a shift in light. The moon was already changing, reverting, paring away the ruby glow. Time not hurried now, it was flying. She traced the horned moon across the flaccid forehead resting at her breast and chanted, 'Hecate, Goddess of the underworlds, lend Douglas strength. Allow this soul to speak the words.' She bowed her head and said, Hecate hear me, hear your humble daughter, your eager acolyte, take my sacrifice given with free will, Hecate hear me.'

Fresh winds were heralded by the voile curtains flapping inward, twisting, twining, misting, trailing further and further beyond their natural length; tendrils spiralled from them as though the air sliced them into whipping threads. Cin continued her chant, louder against the howls waxing in the wind.

Each curtain thread touched the floor, rising upwards and taking a form of its own. Wraiths, swaying in time with her chant, growing sharper as the red-moon receded. Clearly definable faces, ruined faces, ripped and torn with mouths opened in unison, calling, 'Jeno!'

Cin ducked her head so that her ear was close to

Doug's lips, which twitched feebly with a faltering string of syllables. Toothsome numbers falling sweetly from their foulness.

The howling of the wraiths grew as a darkness formed and a woman stepped from their midst. Then all was still.

'Cinthia.' The woman strolled around the table and bent to examine the newly remade corpse. 'Not your best work.'

'Great Hecate, I am ready to give what is yours by right. But...'

Hecate flicked a hand for silence. 'The outcomes of this rite shall be seen as befitting of desires that fuelled them. Return to us. We have need of you.'

'My...' Cin spoke to the dying moonlight alone. Hecate was gone, and with her the soul that had been borrowed.

Cin lowered the empty corpse onto the table. Wraiths howled, sweeping past her as a tangible sickness.

'Cinthia.' Jeno clutching at his face, shrieking like some cursed incantation. 'Cinthia.' he stretched both arms out, feeling the air all around with bloodied hands, his head turning this way and that, desperate to see something, anything, through deeply gouged holes that had held clean blue eyes.

The doors behind him opened and the bodyguards tumbled in to save their master. A mere fractional slice of time later the wraiths had engulfed them all, powering upwards in an ice cold vortex, breaking through ceiling and roof. All the while Jeno squealed for her mercy. The vortex reversed, boring downward through marble and dirt and rock; and still Jeno screamed for Cinthia's pity.

She gave him none. She was intent on searching for her boy. '

'Antony.' She darted forward. Maybe it was not too late? His father's son might remain hers.

The room was a cauldron of blue and green hell fire that belched heat and smoke beyond endurance and forced her back to the step. Then it was gone.

She took a cautious step inside. The room was as it had been; pristine white.

Douglas was gone. And Antony, her boy, lay bloodied on the floor, sightless cavities turned toward her, his mouth mewling his father's words, filled with weakness and lies.

All she had sacrificed was redeemed in full.

She walked into the full moon's silver cast with those glorious numbers tingling on her lips; drawn down with her caress and ripe for the plucking.

# Haiku Quintet: Weather

### Rain

Unremitting – storms
sweep the saturated hills.
And still rivers swell.

### Wind

Many fingered leaves
dropping onto cold water.
Summer's grasp is gone.

### Fog

Hills now lost to view
in fog crowding thick and cold.
Time to light the fire.

### Snow

Crisp and white, snow falls.
Gardens hide beneath its shroud,
waiting for the spring

### Sun

He warms the soil and
tempts fat buds into blossom
with his golden touch

# Grey Magic for Cat Lovers

THERE WAS SOMETHING about a new book that could thrill Kara beyond all else. That satin softness of a pristine dust jacket. That crisp cut closeness of unread pages. That indefinable waft of ink and invitation. Once opened – once the pages had been ruffled through – it could never be so new again.

She was no stranger to impulse buys, but this book was so far out of her comfort zone it almost hurt. It recaptured that sense of the forbidden she hadn't experienced since she'd sneaked strawberries from Granddad's allotment, or prowled the derelict house at the end of Ellie Motsam's street.

Kara reached out to smooth Bug's fur. 'Maybe it's a matter of degrees?' she asked the grey-striped felines. 'When a life is ruled by rules – it goes without saying that any rule breaking is a step in the right direction. Or the wrong one. Hey Bug? Tug?'

Bug yawned and stretched;
Tug merely stared.

Kara knelt by the coffee table to examine the small bronze statue resting at its centre. This had been her first impulse of the week, yanking her out of her predictive academic niche. This statue had *called* to her in the midst of the antiques market.

'I know, Bug. Maybe not called,' she admitted. 'I did keep passing that same stall, though.'

Bug rumbled quietly;
Tug glowered through narrowed eyes.

'Yeah – okay. The seller may have had something to do with it. But give me a break. You don't see Pre-Raphaelite curls on a man so very often. And he was *very* cute.'

Kara picked up the figurine and traced its contours; a woman riding in a chariot, clutching a shawl of feathers around her shoulders, with each rendered in exquisite detail. The work of such a craftsmen had to be a bargain at twenty pounds. It was not the woman, or her cloak, that had first attracted her attention, however. It was the two bullet-headed tomcats pulling the chariot, each with more teeth crammed in their mouths than any animal had a right to; creatures that had tugged at her senses – and her wallet. More statuesque than the tousled felines lounging on her sofa, who were not her cats – but may as well have been.

Her gratis basement flat was a part of the caretaker's wage which paid her way through Uni. It wasn't hard work, seeing cleaners in and out and fielding queries from other tenants in Val's, vast town house. Her most onerous task was to feed and shelter Val's monstrous cats. 'I need you to be a sort of cat au pair,' Val had said. 'They hate being alone, and I'm out of the country so much. I can't possibly put them in a cattery each trip.'

It was rumoured amongst long-term tenants of the

house that this was because every cattery in a twenty mile radius refused to house them a second time, and that was something Kara could well believe. More demanding and devious felines she had yet to come across, and her family had owned a cat or two in their time. And being a sucker for all things *feline*, Val's dire-duo were soon spending their days sprawled on the sofa, whilst Kara herself was relegated to the bean-bag.

She replaced the statue, picked up her glass of Shiraz, and flicked through the book.

*Magic for the Solitary.*

'Solitary what?' she asked Bug.


Bug purred rustily;
Tug slept.


Kara browsed carefully through each heading until one caught her attention. *Change the colour of your eyes.*

She had always felt short-changed over her eyes. Her brother's were ice-blue, like Dad's; her sister's a deep azure; just like Grandma; and Kara's took after Mother in that indeterminate grey/blue of a winter sea. Kara had always envied heroines with eyes that were 'flashing green' or 'chestnut brown' or her own particular favourite; 'limpid violet pools'.

'Anything but sludge-coloured would be good. So waddya think, boys?'


Bug closed his eyes that bit tighter and
pushed his face under one vast paw;
Tug stirred long enough to yawn, sending a wave
of fetid-meat breath in her direction.

Kara waved a hand to disperse the toxic cloud and sighed, knowing not to expect any reaction to anything from Val's venerable moggies – beyond them recognising the sounds of a can opener in use.

She read the page again, curiously, and not a little guiltily.

*This*, she read, *is a glamour to change your appearance and your life. All you need is one pink rose and a red taper candle.*

'Well that sounds simple enough.'

Kate scurried out to the handy climbing rose obscuring the derelict coach house, and was back inside with a good handful in minutes. Shivering from the dusk chill she rammed the blossoms into a vase – selected just one perfect bloom – and laid it next to the book.

'Candles.' She glanced around her. T-lights she had in plenty, and Ikea's scented pillar candles. 'The book says tapers. I must have one somewhere.' She rummaged in various cupboards before unearthing one slightly warped stump of red wax. 'See this, Bug-a-Lug? I knew I had one around somewhere.' She shoved the candle into a holder and lit it.

Bug glared through slitted eyes;
Tug slept.

'Okay what now?' She glanced back at the open book. 'Touch the rose with one hand and the candle with the other and chant, *One two three come for me. One two three change for me. One two three now to thee'*

She waited for a moment or two wondering, with that

semi-atrophied child-part of her mind, if there would be a flash or bang, or some magical sign that something had occurred.

Nothing.

She glanced back at the sofa. 'What do you think, boys? Try again?'

Bug rose up on tiptoes, and hissed:
Tug opened one eye, and glowered.

'Is that a good or a bad? Help me out here.'

Both cats were staring at her now, with fur pleating into Mohican ridges along their backs and tails.

'What?' she demanded.

Bug hissed;
Tug spat.

'What's got up your noses? Wha'sa'matter?' She emptied out her handbag, grabbed for her compact and clicked it open. Her eyes reflecting back at her were a lurid demon red. 'Oh shitting hell. What – have – I – done?'

She ran to the bathroom. The mirror there only emphasised her new look in full-sized crimson glory.

She ran back to the sofa to snatch up the book to re-read the page – and realised her very, very, basic error. *Version two*, she read. *Have ready a candle approximating the colour you wish your eyes to become.*

'Oh fuckin' hell. Oh fuck. Fuck-ity fuck, fuck, fuck!' Kara threw the book at the un-dynamic duo. 'You two are no bloody help. I never thought this shit really worked. What am I going to do? Fuck! Hell! Damn.'

Bug washed his ears;
Tug slept.

'Okay. Keep calm. Colours. Candles. What else have I got?' She rummaged through her kitchen a second time and unearthed a box of partially used tapers from under the sink.

'Most of these are white. No, no. That would be so creepy Kung Fu 'Glasshoppa' eyes. I've got yellow? Nah. Not unless I wanna look like a goat.' She picked out a blue and a green candle stub, badly stained with dust and cat hair, and grimaced as she held them out to the cats. 'No? I didn't think so either. Blotchy is so not a good look.'

The half used deep orange taper she dismissed.

Which left one mauve votive. Kara rubbed the squat wax cylinder on her jeans leg and held it out for inspection.

'Almost violet.' She said to Bug. 'You think?'

Bug curled his pink tongue across his paw
to wash his ragged ears;
Tug went in search of food.

Bracing herself for whatever was to come Kara lit the candle and set a fresh rose from the vase beside it.

'Here goes whatever.' She repeated the chant, willing every fibre of herself into the words. Once again she paused for that sense of difference. And once again the world seemed essentially unchanged.

She grabbed her compact and, taking a deep breath, she clicked it open – peered at herself – and exhaled slowly.

'Liz Taylor? Eat your heart out.' She admired the effect, turning her face this way and that to see all of her small, round reflection; and finally blew herself a kiss. 'This I can live with. Irises that are, well, iris coloured.'

She picked up the book and fanned the pages. Not reading it, nor even noting what was breezing past her newly made-over eyeballs. Her mind was flickering over the possibilities faster than anyone could ever read.

She picked up the compact and checked once again.

She went to the bathroom and checked in the decent-sized mirror.

She leaned across the sink and prised her lids apart, one eye, and then the other. Her irises remained steadfastly lavender. 'Not violet as such,' she mused. 'But near as damn it. And nothing's changed back. Yet. It really has worked.'

Back to the sitting room. She plopped into the still-warm space vacated by Tug. 'What now, Bug? What would you choose?'

Bug yawned and stretched a paw to tap her thigh;
  Tug glowered, slit-eyed, from the kitchen door.

'New body to go with the eyes?' she chuckled, gently detaching Bug's scythe-like claws from her jeans and leaned down to retrieve the book.

'There's this one. *A spell to lose weight.* Says I need vanilla and jasmine oils, a blue quartz crystal and a large slice of cake. *No diet required. Bury the cake and watch your pounds melt away as the cake decays.*' She stared at the page, pursing her lips. 'Well I've always got cake handy. I've got Vanilla *essence* in the kitchen, and there's winter jasmine in the garden. They're close. Can't hurt. Right? I mean if it doesn't work, I can still diet the hard way.'

It should have made her feel so right. Yet it felt so very wrong. 'For every action there is an equal and opposite reaction,' she said to Bug. She scratched at his tattered ears and stared at the page. 'What can it hurt? It's one slice of chocolate cake I won't be eating. And if it works? I will be so good. I swear – I will never snack again.'

Bug sneezed;
Tug leapt onto the sofa arm, and growled.

*

Two months later Kara sorted through her wardrobe for something to wear that did not fall off her newly svelte hips. She cinched her jeans in at the waist. It would get her as far as the Mall.

'Forty pounds! Wow! Looks like I'll be shopping for new clothes *yet again*.' She looked around her and sighed. Talking to Bug and Tug was a habit she had got used to. It made talking to herself seem marginally less insane. As neither cat had put in an appearance this morning she had only her reflection to advise her. Val must be home, she thought. At least I get use of my sofa back for a day or two.

A glance in the mirror told her she was good to go with or without the cats' approval and four hours later she was sitting in the Boundary Book Store's *Coffee Stop*, with a mound of boutique bags shoved under the table.

Size eight. Eight! She thought, and suppressed a whoop of triumph.

The past weeks had been an odd experience. The oddest thing being how no one noted her twenty-five percent shrinkage in body mass. The new Kara was accepted as if she had always been this slim, lithe, creature. Even her closest friends had not commented beyond, 'you're looking good today' or, 'did you get some coloured contacts?'

Whilst people said nothing of the *new Kara*, Kara noticed a gradual change in how she came to be treated.

Angie, the queen bi-atch, had been unusually nice. 'Invited me on one of her girlie nights out,' she told the cats one evening. 'I've arrived – apparently.'

Bug had yawned;
Tug had blinked slowly and looked away.

Man-hunting with Amazonian Ang, among the clubs of Broad Street, was something many of her class saw as so cool; inclusion apparently essential for some. Kara had never been one of those willing to gnaw off her own leg for admittance to that Court, but she surprised herself, nevertheless, when she declined the royal command. And her rebellion that made her feel so achingly superior.

Now she sat in the Coffee Stop, with a new wardrobe of clothes around her feet, getting the kind of signals from the guys at the next table she had never fielded in her life before. She was looking good, and she knew it.

Kara winked, before turning back to her mocha and

Danish. Things are looking up, she thought. Just proves – I do NOT need Angela Cartwright's help to pull.

She fished for her purse. *For every action there is an equal and opposite reaction*, she thought, as she had several times in past weeks. The weight loss had been a rapid and constant action and the opposite reaction she noticed most was how pounds sterling were dropping away at the same alarming rate. Her cards were maxed out, she had just drawn twenty pounds from the cash machine, and had her card retained, and a quick count in her wallet showed twenty four pounds and change to her name.

Glancing through the doors, she could see the rows of bookshelves.

And she wondered.

Her magic book came from here. It was tempting. She had not tried any further incantations since her weight loss spell. Partly because *Casting Health & Happiness* had little to offer now she had the 'bod', but mostly because she was wary about how permanent, and how safe, it would prove to be.

She patted her flat stomach and flashed her 'violet eyes' at the 'hottie-guys'. She wasn't seriously interested, but it felt good watching them vie for her attention.

Her thoughts were more drawn to her wallet. Her car insurance was due. Then there were her mobile charges, never mind food and petrol.

Kara finished her snack, gathered her bags and rode the in-store escalator down to the *Mind, Body & Spirit* section. Won't hurt to look see, she thought. Something to tide me over.

She browsed for a long while, not wanting to

squander what little she had. Desperation kept her scanning the same shelves time and again, feeling that she had seen every spine a hundred times, but 'knowing' that when the right book came under her hand– she would feel it. So when her hand paused over that single, slim, copy she could not believe how she had missed it every other time. She did not doubt, however, that this was the one.

*Wealth & Destiny.*

Its cover showed a blue-grey goat, chest deep in water, with its reflection shimmering below it like some Caprinan court card.

The closing bell rang.

She shelled out half her remaining resources without a second thought and headed for home.

*

Kara was barely through her front door before she was scrabbling through her latest book-buy. Page flipping grew more desperate as spell after spell asked for things she did not have, couldn't afford to buy, or in some cases could barely identify. 'Black snake root, galangal root, tonka beans. Where the hell would I buy those, even if I *did* know what they where,' she muttered at Bug and Tug as they wound around her legs in feline supplication. She fed them and headed for the sitting room with her post.

She wished she hadn't bothered as she eyed her latest heap of bills. 'There's course fee payments on top of this lot.' She sighed, turning the page on yet another incantation intended for *paying an urgent bill*.

'I got those first spells by winging it, didn't I boys? What if I went through the book to see what I've got in the house that matches – and go from there? That's not being a cheapskate. It's just a case of desperate measures.'

She reviewed the spells from a different perspective. After twenty minutes she had a depressingly short list. Most of the herbs and spices on it she had in her kitchen. But the incantations promising the biggest and fastest results also had the weirdest ingredients; and that required money she simply did not have.

'Which,' she said, 'is sort of the whole point.'

Bug strolled past her, sat on the sofa,
and cleaned his whiskers;
Tug joined him.

'So what *can* I get for next to nothing?' she asked them. 'What about these chicken's feet?' She waved the list under their noses.

Bug rumbled and pushed the paper away;
Tug snoozed.

'No? I suppose you're right. Tesco birds never have feet. And I'm not creeping around a farmyard looking for chickens to slaughter.'

She stared at the page for a long while, gnawing at her thumbnail, pondering the ramifications. There was one item that cost least – and more importantly – promised much.

'*Dirt from an un-consecrated grave.*'

'It says if I leave a coin in its place its harms none. But an un-consecrated grave?' She glanced up at the windows and saw it was getting late. 'I know where, Bug. But I really need to think on this one.'

*

It was Saturday before Kara could get to the field in daylight. She stood on the edge and frowned at the trio of ancient burial mounds she had studied recently with her class. Formal burials, consecrated by rites, yet not in the Churchyard sense that her book implied; she hoped.

'And needs be,' she told herself.

The history student within her was offended at an act of sheer vandalism. Yet that same historian argued that the power was an intrinsic part of death rites – which included the grave. 'And the warrior chief under here? I bet he'd be dead chuffed to think he's still got the power,' she told herself. 'Wouldn't he?'

Kara climbed the nearest mound and paused to scan the surrounding fields and road. It would not go well with the faculty if one of their students got herself arrested whilst desecrating a designated ancient monument. All was quiet and still, not so much as a bike passing along the road below her.

Kneeling, she unwrapped her trowel – and chopped a square of turf – and laid it carefully to one side – and stared at the grassless patch.

'Madness,' she muttered. 'Sheer madness. Forgive me.'

The trowel plunged into the exposed soil and emptied a shower of the potent loam into a waiting bag. Soil that was dark and damp and crumbling.

Kara pulled a broken Roman coin from her pocket. It was all she had that was anything near old enough and she wondered; would a Viking warrior would be offended by its connotations? Muttering a short prayer to all the various gods she thought might be involved she dropped it into the newly excavated hole, and, after a small hesitation, added a modern coin, just in case. Firming the turf back into place she scuttled away.

*

Kara was not sure if darkness was necessary. It just seemed to feel right. If nothing else it made the candle light more atmospheric.

She moved the furniture back and set out a wide circle of salt. Not quite the nine feet across that the book required, but close enough to be usable, she decided. She set tea lights in a mixture of green and red holders around the circle.

She sat cross legged at the centre, her coffee table altar set across one side, and checked her list. 'One pot with grave soil and small green candle. Check. One goddess statue. Check. One lottery ticket – for tonight's rollover? Cheee-eck!'

From here on Kara was in uncharted territory. The book had said *keep it simple. The most important part is that, once begun, the practitioner(s) should keep their chant constant until the focus candle burns fully out. And then to be patient and wait.*

It did sound simple on paper. Kara waved her hands across the selection, breathing out and then in, and began.

Two words, over and over and over.

'Money me, money me, money me.'

Within minutes her lips began to stumble. Dry and aching her tongue stuck to the roof of her mouth. The simple phrase began to hum within her chest, reverberating through her skull, singing through every tooth, every digit, every hair.

And all the while the green candle burned downward.

At some point she was aware of Bug and Tug strolling in to take up their accustomed spots on the sofa. She could feel their eyes on her, could swear they were humming with her, but she dared not look, or stop to listen. She was starting to feel light-headed, eyes unfocussed, extremities tingling, before the flame spluttered. The fine tilth had begun to mingle with wax around the wick as it guttered – and finally died.

'So mote it be,' she whispered.

She waited.

Nothing.

Ten long minutes. Nothing.

Kara glanced at the sofa.

Bug yawned;
Tug got up, and slowly walked away.

'Conditions normal, eh Bug?' She rose stiffly and stepped out of the circle. She switched on her laptop and Googled the National Lottery. Time to see what had occurred. If anything.

Ticking off the sixth number on her ticket was an anti-climax.

One had been a thrill, two heart stopping, three the pinnacle – by ball four she knew she was on her way.

Kara looked down at the winning slip, numb with the wonder of what she had achieved.

'Fucking hell. It's only bloody worked!'

Bug stared;
Tug was not there.

She glanced at the table-altar within its circle of salt, at a loss to know what she had done or how.

'If it really was as easy as following directions in a New-Age book, wouldn't everyone be doing it? Coincidence?' she asked the Bug. 'It can't be that easy. So what did I do right?'

Bug yowled;
Tug remained absent.

Realisation came slowly. Bug was not howling at *her*, but at spot somewhere past her left shoulder.

She stared with him. Squinting along his line of sight she could discern a vague shimmer, like a heat haze over summer tarmac. It wavered – began to take shape. A man-shape. Long and well built. And, she realised, ominously Norse looking.

'Oh shit. This does not look good.'

In less than a minute Kara had a full blown Viking warrior lying within her salt circle. A sword clutched at his breast, shield under his feet, a folded wolf's skin under his head. He wore a heavy, bronze, helm, and at his side hung a large silver tipped cow-horn. She noted all this detail with the detached interest of an historian. The saner half of her brain proceeded to gibber with the shocked awe of any mortal faced with the business end of a Viking burial in her living room.

He was so perfectly formed. Blonde hair was tied back in neat braids; his beard was delicately trimmed and plaited. His clothes clean and apparently new. His sword grip seemed well used – the sheath stained here and there, its strapping much repaired. The blade she could not yet see.

'Oh fuck it. I've really screwed up this time, Bug. What in hell am I going to do?'

Bug growled;
the Viking stirred and moaned.

The Viking sat up. He was grasping at his right shoulder, rotating his arm, checking it for movement. He looked around him. His gaze fixed on Kara. He croaked a few Norse words, swallowed and few times and repeated them more firmly.

Kara shook her head. Reading texts in class was one thing. Hearing that language, in a deep voice, creaky from disuse, really was another. She felt for Bug, seeking any comfort to be had from any truly living being, even if it were some scraggy Methuselahean cat.

Bug yowled;
the Viking spoke – English.

'Speak Woman. I command this. Speak.'
'Uh, hi?' She waggled her fingers limply.
'What is this place?'
'My house. Well not mine exactly but I live here.'
'I was in the Halls with my kin.' He bounded to his feet and lunged.

Kara drew back, and blew out hastily drawn breath as the Viking was halted violently at the salt-ring edge.

He ripped off his helm, spitting a few muttered curses that Kara did not quite catch, and was staring around the circle – utter disdain curling his lips. 'Witch,' he hissed. 'Witch!'

'Um. Yeah. I guess that would be me. Sort of.'

'You guess? You would know such. A woman of your years.'

'I'm new at this magic stuff. And I'm not that old!' She stepped closer to eye him angrily. Here she was all violet eyes, and really great figure, and who the hell did he think he was talking too?

'I am no whelp,' he said. 'And you must have studied long to achieve this, Witch. To snatch me from the Halls. You can be no maiden.'

He lunged again, his hand crashing into the unseen barrier with a hollow *whomp*. The Viking rubbed at his fist and glared at her. 'Witch,' he hissed again.

'Yeah, so you keep saying,' Kara said. She walked around the edge of the circle, examining her trophy with what she hoped was an historian's eye. Musing not only on the wonder of seeing the real thing, but also at how accurate the re-enactment brigade were with colours and style. 'Thing is,' she went on. 'I said I'm a little new at this. So when I say I have no idea what we can do. I mean it.'

'Let me go, woman. Release me. Let me return to the Halls of my Father.'

'I would if I could. If I knew how. This was an accident. I didn't mean to drag you here.' She slid a cautious foot forward and dabbed at the salt ring.

The Viking gasped, and fell to one knee.

'Oooh. I was afraid of that,' she said. 'Basic physics.

Can't make mass from nothing. So you can't exist. Not in any real sense. If I were to rub this out you would go with it. So we have a problem. Or you do at any rate.'

Bug yowled;
Tug stalked in and sat yowling beside him.

'Your familiars disagree,' the Viking snarled. 'What do they say, Witch?'

'Haven't the slightest idea. Wish I did,' she replied.

'Bygul is merely greeting Trjegul.' Val, appeared through the French doors. 'They are brothers and seldom apart. Rather sweet, isn't it?' She paused to eye the Viking up and down. 'My goodness, Kara. Tug said it was urgent and he wasn't wrong. You do seem to have summoned up a problem for yourself.' She peered closely at the man's face. 'It has been a long while, Torstein Alfrsun.'

'My Lady.' Torstein fell to his knees and bowed his head. 'Forgive me. I did not break your rules willingly. I waited in the Halls, feasting with my kin. I waited for Ragnarok.'

'And poof. You were somewhere else?'

'Well, yes.'

Val flicked a hand toward him and his mouth snapped shut. 'We shall have to get you back, shan't we? Can't have you rampaging around before time, corporeal or no. And you!' she spun around to point at Kara. 'You have been dabbling!'

'I didn't mean anything. I never imagined it would work. I was playing around.'

'Obviously.' Val looked at the coffee table, and her

whole demeanour changed from mildly exasperated to one of iron and flint. Reaching in, past the salt-locked barrier, she picked up the statuette. 'Where did you get this?' she demanded.

'Flea market.' Kara stammered.

'From whom?'

'What?'

'The seller. Who was it?'

'No idea. A guy.'

'Tall? Young? Curly red hair? Scar?' she drew a finger across her lip. 'Handsome?'

Kara cast her mind back and realised she had no clear image of the seller. 'Why would I remember,' she replied. 'It was just a statue, but yeah. Red hair I think. Youngish maybe. Hard to tell.'

'Oh yes. That's him. It would only ever be him' Val nodded grimly. Tucking the statue under one arm she held her hand out to gesture at the waiting cats.

Bygul, now taller than the arm of Kara's sofa, got up
and walked out through the French window;
Trjegul, followed.

'But...' Kara stared after them. 'This is not happening.'

'Oh, it's happening, unfortunately.' Val signalled to Torstein. 'You will come with me – again.'

'Mighty Freya.' he held his hands to her. 'I cannot move beyond the Witch's band.'

'You will very soon.' Val bent to gather a pinch of salt and sprinkled it over his head. 'Outside. Now. My chariot awaits.'

'But, you're Val. Just Val. Everyone knows that,' Kara said.

'Val is more of a pet name,' Val replied. 'Names change. I am Val, yes, and I am Freya, and I am the essence of the Valkyrie. Names can be so misleading. But you, my dear,' She smiled suddenly and beckoned. 'You, Kara, will fit right in with the one that you already have. Come.'

'Now?' Kara looked at the crumpled lottery ticket still clasped in her hand. 'With respect, bugger off. I just won. This is my dream, Val. Or whatever your name is. It's millions. It's enough to … I don't know. Do anything. It's more money than any poor bastard like me could ever earn!'

'Money?' Val took the slip and touched it against a tea light until blue and yellow tongues of flame licked across it toward her fingers. 'Money? Sister, where you're going, trust me, you will not be needing it.'

# Corinna's Reply

(In answer to Marlowe's translation of Ovid's *Amores*)

Tarmac bubbles in a midday street.
I open the door, and step into
a gloomy twilight, behind drawn curtains.
That dawn/dusk state,
which hides his intent—
or so he thinks.

Stealthy, catlike, I slink past.
But his hand is the snake,
with fangs to snag my hem.
Buttons part. Cloth hits the floor.
Still I wear more then he—
and more than he would wish.

An early shift left me slicked with sweat,
hair clinging to a clammy face and neck.
It shields my eyes
and hides my irritation.
Were I Cleopatra or Cynthia Payne—
would he notice? Would he care?

He's on his feet, in all his glory, glowing
in the gloom; slowly rising to attention.
His eyes glitter, his lips pout.
Who does he think he is!

I give in with poor grace—
or I'll have no peace.

Afternoons such as this…
are not rare enough!

# Mayday Comes Askew

A FRESH BREEZE rustled the flimsy drapes hung across the windows and Flora closed her eyes, revelling in the cool air drying her freshly cleaned nakedness. It felt good to be alive and in this glorious form.

'Samya.'

The Temple-maiden hurried to kneel at her feet, and shuffled awkwardly to keep pace with Flora's pacing to and fro.

'Oh get up for Juno's sake. Stop that grovelling and just listen. What can you hear?'

'Nothing Ma'am.'

'No. Nor can I. Belenus' rites should be in full fire and frolic mode so why is it so damnably quiet out there?'

'Ma'am?' Samya hesitated. This mistress was prone to instant retributions for the slightest wrong. The smaller deities could be that way, she found, and as a Ritual Supervisor she'd been sent to prepare them all over the eons.

'Have you heard anything in the markets, Samya? Is Mankind in flux yet again? Who has been stirring them up this time? Has Febris sent another plague down there? Or has that poser Mars started yet another war? That boy enjoys playing soldiers far too much. Just because he's Jupiter's lad he thinks he can do what he likes.'

She glanced down at Samya. 'Oh, I don't expect you to know. But you girls usually hear the rumours in temple long before we have the facts.' Flora waved a hand, exasperated albeit resigned. 'Jupiter would do so much better if he had a proper palace, like Zeus has. But no. He had to hang out in Rome – had to be *in touch with his people* – for all the good that did him.'

Samya shifted, uncomfortable.

*

'Yes, I know. Juno is your ruler. Come to that Juno is Jupiter's ruler.' She sighed and reached out to touch the woman's shoulder. 'I shouldn't say things like that should I? Juno is our great Goddess. I wouldn't want any argument with her. And if I did disagree I'm not stupid enough to say it in anyone's hearing. Oh, stand up, woman. I do hate talking to the top of people's heads. Now. Tell me all.'

Samya hauled herself to her feet and shuffled for a moment or two, reluctant to be the bringer of potentially ill portents. 'Well it's only a rumour mind, but I've heard it said by one of the Temple-maids that does for her, that Eostre's following had such a downturn this season she took it up with Jupiter. Meaning no offence, your worshipfulness.'

'A small turn out?' Flora grinned. She had never liked the way that Eostre dominated the spring rites when Spring was all about flowers in her book. Hearing that she'd had a bad Rite was cheering. 'Poor dear. She never mentioned it at Juno's last gathering. Not that she would I suppose. Not the sort of thing a deity likes to boast about. What came of it?'

'We maidens never heard no more Ma'am.'

'Really? How odd. I thought you Temple-maids knew everything.' Flora stared at the horizon that had yet to show a hint of dawn. Plenty of time, yet there remained a restlessness tickling at her core. It gnawed at her. Uncertainty was not something she was used to. Was she imagining it? Were the sounds from below lacking somehow? Now that she concentrated it was quite definitely quieter than it should be. Samya's comments hadn't helped. If the Maidens were talking about poor turnouts then perhaps it would be wise to arrive a little ahead of time. Give her priestesses a reason to whip in the stragglers.

She glanced again at her mirrored wall and smoothed her hands over well balanced hips. Her reflection was comforting. The coming day was one of duty, demanding the most from her physical splendour, and she saw suitable perfection. Flora dreaded a time when she might find herself turned into a wrinkled crone. 'Always had the edge on Eostre,' she posed, admiring her slim ankles and full bust. 'She needs to get her acolytes in order. Talking of which, isn't it time we got ready?'

Clapping her hands briskly Samya called the bevy of Temple-maids to bring Flora's gown. It took them a while to rap and tuck its pale folds around the goddess' svelte body. They flitted around her in a trembling dance, primping and tweaking her clothes, twirling her gold tresses into long ringlets, dabbing her face with powders, touching colour around her eyes, daubing scent on her earlobes and cleavage, fixing garlands of flowers to body and head in honour of her name. Then they dispersed like a cloud of dowdy moths to allow the butterfly loose from their midst, and finally Flora advanced through the clouds stepping down from her sky-born temple to view her subjects.

May-eve was over and all of the fires of Beltaine would be re-kindled, as custom demanded. Once on her descent the quiet of the day was all too obvious. There were spots of fire here and there but nothing near how it should be.

Her musings were cut short however. Belenus was drifting up toward her and had halted, lurking in the mists of between and waiting. His eye met hers with a tinge of lust in their corners; an insufferable leer of knowing. She sighed.

He was still watching her, silent, expectant, and did she detect a hint of uncertainty? She hesitated, wondering what he had left for her to contend with. It was nothing she had not seen before she was certain. Nothing was so base that she had not seen its like a dozen times before. She was, after all, of Roman stock. Belenus was a mischievous one and he had been in these islands far longer than she, but how she hated the undisciplined rites of Beltaine Eve.

'What he really needs is a few more priests. Careless of him if he's lost what he had.' She smiled grimly at her own part on that. She and Belenus had shared this day for a very long time, but it was all they had in common.

She straightened her spine and swept past him without a word. This was her grand entrance. Flora, Goddess of fruit and flower had stepped into the mortal world. Where were the maypoles? All strung with ribbons and streamers? Where were the flower garlands for young girls and boys to throw around their lovers of the hour? The music and the dancing and merrymaking with so much food and drink?

She glanced back at Belenus. What had that uncouth Celt done? If this was one of his course jokes.

Belenus only shrugged a wordless reply, a small spark of pity and commiseration in his gaze.

Flora descended a little further to view one particular village green with its church and tiny straggle of houses. Annual revelries had taken place on this very spot since it was little more than a clearing in the ancient forest.

Looking up and down the swathe of grass she felt a frisson of panic rippling out through her assurance. There was nothing, and more importantly, no one in sight. She searched further afield, following the dirt road for a mile in both directions for her followers. Returning to the green that was now lit by early sun she pondered on exactly what might be amiss. True, no tangible sacrifice had been made to her in recent years, and granted, the licentious excesses of the past were not adhered to as they once had been, but she had always counted on at least a fayre and the erection of dancing poles to keep her memory alive.

Her eyes were drawn back to the church. There in the doorway stood a preacher. The sombre black of his attire was broken only by pristine white collar and cuffs and by a brown leather prayer book clutched tightly in his hands. He stood guard over the green, seeming to dare his flock to gather on this day.

'These Christians've been edging us out for years. Now they've been and got rid've all the fun.'

Flora started at the sound of Belenus' gravely voice in her ear. 'Don't be silly,' she said. 'They love maypoles.

It's all the fun some of them have.'

'Not anymore. Maypoles 're not allowed. 'Tis the law I'm told.'

'Law?' she said. 'What human law can prevent it? I will have my due obeisance's. None of us will survive in this world without them.'

'Cromwell his name is.' Belenus replied. 'Banned all of the feasting. They're only allowed prayers 'n stuff, even for the Yule-tide.' He sniffed loudly, wiping his nose on his hairy arm. 'Odin's not very happy.'

He really was a handsome god, but that did not stop him being a disgusting reprobate. Earthy, Ceridwen called him. Uncouth was Flora's assessment. She swallowed convulsively and resisted the temptation to comment; waiting impatiently for him to continue.

'Gone.' He said sadly. 'All gone. Yule, Hallows Eve, Spring and Summer Solstice, the whole lot. Seems this Cromwell struck a deal with powers that be, some kind of long-term lease on humanity. We're being taken from the calendar until further notice.'

'All of us?' she whispered in horror.

He nodded.

'But why weren't we warned?' she demanded. 'It's atrocious. They can't strike us off, just like that!' She snapped her fingers under his nose. 'We have the right to seek our own mortal servants.'

'It's happened,' he replied gloomily. 'What can you do? Or any of us?' He looked toward the north and west of the island. 'I've still got a few corners left,' he mused, 'Celts are Celts, whatever happens to the rest of the world; and always will be. They don't hold with all this abstinence. But I'm thinking you've got some real problems young maid, what with Rome falling and things.'

'Well we shall see about that,' she replied, turning on her heels to march back toward the mist. 'They can't do it. Jupiter!' she screamed, 'We need to speak!'

# Time's Excuses

Time pulls down curtains of indifference
for infernal conscience to hide beyond.
Memory fails in convenient places
and blows in clammy mists on demand.
Common sense dictates the failure rate
for synapses to connect or respond.
But pride papers over cracks of guilt
that forbidden motives leave behind.

# Midnight Twilight

LAND OF THE MIDNIGHT Sun? Not quite how Ellie would have put it. Even though that sultry, red-gold light source hanging heavy on the horizon really was the sun and it really was midnight.

Her editor had said 'If your eyesight's good enough you can read a book outdoors at one in the morning.' Intriguing, maybe, but Ellie couldn't help feeling it wasn't much of a pitch. She could do that back home if the moon was full enough. She had envisaged more than this tinted gloom.

Ellie could have coped with the light levels for the single month she'd be here to research the researchers. It was the dammed sled dogs waking her just after twelve each 'night' that exhausted her. Tonight she had managed just two hours before the howling had begun.

She pulled the quilt past her nose and revelled in the sudden heat of her trapped breath.

'You want to go tramping around in the ice?' her boss had told her. 'We're into silly season and we've got another Global Emissions summit coming up. I want a 'climate research stations paid for by oil conglomerates' expose. Or anything else you can dig up. That's your brief. You want to do this Sasquatch thing while you are at it? Fine. But make your expense account pay for once.'

After begging for an assignment that was more

challenging, this was starting to feel more punishment than prize. Except that her Modern Myths of the World by-line couldn't afford to pass up this new spate of whispered reports once they were out there in the conspiracy universe. The 'Sasquatch of the Arctic' rumour needed looking into if only because no one else had yet done so. She had wondered why that had been. Now she knew. 'Because nobody else was this stupid,' she muttered, breathing out heavily to raise the temperature another nano-degree. The howling rose a notch. Ellie waited for any signs that the 'residents' were going to go and check it out. Nothing stirred, which was weird. That Apsel guy was usually so manic over his precious dogs.

'Fuck it.' She twitched back the quilts and slid from the bunk's clinging warmth to peer through the window. Nothing out of place, but as she could see little beyond the cabin opposite that proved very little. She looked at her watch. Almost 1.00 a.m. Ellie hauled on her parka, boots and gloves, remembering to grab the ever-present rifle from its hooks by the main door, and went outside. The tethered dog team was the best indicator of any intrusion, and the animals were not bothered by anything within the camp perimeter. Their attention was riveted on the tundra and, as always, no ordering from Ellie would quieten them. She walked past the dogs to the edge of the camp, watching the horizon with its deeply tinted dawn-dusk light.

'It's downright bloody unnerving, is what it is,' she called back to them, the only ears to hear her. Several members of the pack looked in her direction without missing either howl or yip. 'Six stocky, stiff-legged,

Spitzen sled-dogs,' she said, 'salivating savagely at the sun.' She wandered back to make soothing noises at them, though being careful to keep out of their reach.

The Research Head, Dr Hiegel, had been very clear on that. 'These are not pets, my dear,' he'd assured her when she arrived. 'They're one step away from the wolf, and every team is a pack. If Apsel is not here don't touch them. In fact, don't touch them if he *is* here. The man's almost as savage as his beasts.'

It didn't inspire confidence. And was a gross exaggeration as it turned out, because the dogs were not unfriendly toward her, merely indifferent. Not the ravening hell hounds that Hiegel had inferred.

Apsel was a different matter.

'What in hell these people want you lot here for is beyond me,' she said to the nearest dog. It stopped barking long enough to snarl, making Ellie take a rapid step back. 'I've read the figures. More sled dogs in Finnmark than humans. Except these guys here have skidoos. They've got radios and mobile phones and internet. They could call for a rescue team anytime. Plus it's heading toward high summer. What in hell *do* they need you guys for?'

The shaggy, grey-coated Spitz glanced toward her, tail wafting, before pointing its snout towards the ice flow. The snarl gave way to a quiet whine.

'What is it, girl? Bears?' Ellie said, and snorted back a quick laugh. 'This place is getting to me. I'm starting to sound like a Lassie repeat.' The dog looked back at her, licking nervously at its lips. The gesture was out of character for such a stoic matriarch which, Apsel had assured Ellie, was the best lead dog he'd ever had. As befitted its role, the dog's ice-blue eyes showed only disdain for the camp and everyone in it.

Ellie peered across the open expanse and sighed. 'We've got to stop meeting this way. People will talk.'

The dog whined, paddled its front feet, and uttered a few short yips.

'What's that, girl? You say a little girl fell down a mine shaft? Or just more bears?' She wrapped her arms around herself, fighting against a sudden shudder. 'Bears. God, I hope not.' She remembered last week's bear visit all too vividly. When the storeroom door was ripped up and scattered across the ice, before Apsel could send the beast on its way with a volley of rifle fire.

Away in the half-light she could swear something moved; way, way off where the hills opened into an icy plateau. Without field glasses she couldn't be certain. It was unsettling, because the only things of that size out there were polar bears. And those she could do without. Whatever it was had seemingly moved on because the dogs were returning to their rest; quiet now but for the odd snarl as the lead dog claimed priority.

The almost-silence that followed was as unnerving as the almost-dark, with just the *tink* and *crack* of distant ice, and the occasion whirring of wind between the cabins.

Once, she thought, the ice wouldn't have melted this far north. Once, this tiny valley, rising way about sea level, would never have bared its rocky face to the sky, but would remain secreted within its permanent, blue-white ice shell.

'But that's why I'm here,' she said. 'The Big Meltdown. Anything else is gravy.'

She let herself back into the cabin, racked the gun, and

entered the galley in search of coffee; lighting the propane stove and settling the kettle as quietly as she could.

'Maybe coffee's not the best thing for the sleepless.' Apsel leaned against the doorjamb, tousled and bleary, his quilt wrapped around him in place of his parka.

'And yet here we are,' Ellie replied. She smiled at him, over-cheery perhaps, but he was a hard man to nail for an interview. This might be her only chance. All of the research team had been more than happy to talk, mostly to debunk everything she asked them, and she expected no less. These were scientists, measurers of rocks and winds and ice temperatures – and scientists who were reluctant to make a public statement on their funding – let alone anything Fortean, whatever their private thoughts. Apsel's reluctance was totally different, and Ellie could not work out if it was personal or just antipathy toward strangers in general. She pulled another mug toward the kettle. 'Want some?'

He nodded. 'You fixing to go out again, Miss?'

'Something disturbed the dogs. I went out to see.'

'They do that sometimes, this time of year. They don't like when they can't see the moonlight.' He frowned, scratching at his bird's-nest beard.

Ellie smiled at his fractured English. It was something she found hard to get used to. 'Don't they get used to the twilight?' she said.

He shrugged, not quite meeting her eye. She wasn't buying it. 'They saw something out there. I know they did.' She poured water on the dried coffee grains, slowly to give herself thinking space. 'And I saw something out there. It was moving north. A sled, I think.' She watched his face carefully for the merest hint of expression in those weather-worn features, but there was nothing. 'You do know why I'm here?' she said. 'There've been rumours.'

He nodded. Sharp yet reluctant. There it was. The chink in Apsel's defence.

'So what do you think? Is there something in it? Do we have an Arctic Sasquatch?'

'Stallo?' he grinned, his flat features suddenly animated. 'You want a story for the young ones? You tell them about them Stallo. Big things. Fierce.'

'Stallo are some kind of Troll, right?' She shook her head. 'I'm not talking old folk tales. I'm talking of genuine sightings going back over the past fifty years or more.'

'You think maybe those tales only come from the old days? Like we don't get new ones?'

'Good point,' Ellie said. 'So what do you think about these sightings? Have you seen anything? You're out here more than most.'

Apsel's smile snapped off, his face shifting back to the inscrutable blank that seemed to be his default setting. 'I think maybe bears,' he said finally. 'We got bears. Plenty of bears, you know? Like last week.' He waved in the general direction of the storage shack. 'Don't go outside without that gun, lady. Or better, don't go out on your own at all in the dark.'

'That gives me plenty of time. The sun's always up.' She pushed a mug of black coffee across the table and watched him spoon in mounds of whitener and sugar.

'Lady, just about anything up here is a hunter. And hunters, they know a straggler when they see one.

Stragglers are weak. They're the prey. Just saying. My job's keeping you people safe. Cold in here,' he added. 'Going to get some sleep now.' He picked up the mug and headed for his bunk without another word.

Ellie slapped her fingers against the edge of the counter. She knew she'd handled that badly, half asleep and too eager for answers. Somehow she didn't think Apsel was ever going to give up the things he knew easily. Instead he patronised her. 'Moron. His sodding dogs keep me awake and it's nothing to do with him? I'll leave them for the bloody bears next time.' She shovelled sugar into her coffee and stirred until it slopped. She hadn't been a journo this long without getting to spot a lie. She paused, watching the brown vortex swirl a few tiny bubbles around the epicentre. 'Well, maybe I'll get that story after all.'

The next night, at 12.30 sharp when the Spitzen began their yammering, Ellie was prepared. Fully dressed, she only had to put on her boots and collect the gun before she slipped out into the crepuscular night.

The dogs barely acknowledged her as she emerged. She knew it was no use trying to *shush* them. A stranger such as herself, once deemed harmless, was ignored.

Ellie crossed the cleared paths to the edge of the camp and scanned the snow covered slopes and dips, adjusting her binoculars time and again, but she saw nothing. Maybe Apsel had it. Those stupid mutts could just be barking at the sun.

A noise from the cabin made her glance back, expecting one of the team to come after her. No-one emerged, though the dogs' noise was cut short.

Looking back to the horizon she spotted that same

fleeting shadow from the previous night. Through her glasses it took form.

'Not a bear,' she said. 'Not unless they've mastered sledding without the world's notice. Okay, so what is some guy doing driving a sled across the wastes this far out? There's nothing out there but the cold.' She watched until the sled vanished into the shadows of distance before she retreated to the cabin for the inevitable coffee.

For two more nights she was woken in that same hour between twelve and one by the dogs; and each night she saw the same sled, moving along the same trail.

*

When she asked who else had seen it the scientific team were, in turn, amused, exasperated, and as downright patronising as the taciturn Apsel. Ellie wasn't surprised. If she'd heard someone claiming to see the same sledder heading across the tundra at the same time every night, she would probably have laughed with them. She might have toyed with the idea of a story, but she'd have laughed.

MYSTERY SLEDDER ON MIDNIGHT TUNDRA.

It was a real *Sunday Sport* headline.

Apsel gave her one of 'those' looks and left the room before she could get around to him.

'Which makes me wonder one thing,' she told Hiegel, 'if it's the same guy every night how come he's always going in the same direction? He has to come back, unless he's got some weird kind of arctic circuit training thing going?'

Hiegel had laughed her off and demanded she kept to her brief.

'We deal in facts Miss Levin. If you wanted fairy tales

there are any number of Father Christmas camps in the region. Perhaps it's Santa out on a practice run?'

She was met with that same derision from the rest of his team. She was used to that. An interest in unknown phenomenon came with that baggage. She tried a few more runs at Apsel and was systematically blanked every time. That just clinched it. There was something here, and she could not – *would* not – ignore it.

At just past midnight she was waiting, kitted up in all weather gear and short-skis. Right on cue the dogs began to twitch and moan, padding back and forth, licking nervously at each others' muzzles and sending anxious glances towards the horizon. It was only a minute or two before they began to point noses to the sky and howl. She pushed off in the general direction of the sled's path.

It took her a few minutes to get into stride. Langrenn – cross-country skiing – was not a sport she knew well, but it wasn't so hard once she got the rhythm. Distances, she knew, were deceptive in deserts, whether they were made of sand or ice and she had travelled for a quarter of an hour, legs and arms pumping in unison whilst keeping her breathing slow and even, before she stopped to ensure her target was on the same trail as on previous nights.

He was. He seemed to be so sure of himself, skirting the edges of the vanishing ice, urging his team occasionally to 'Gee' and 'Haw', but mostly to 'Hike! Hike!' in a bellowing roar. These words she picked out across the expanse because she knew them. Now and then other words that she could not catch drifted in. Names, maybe?

Another few minutes and she stopped; glancing back

to make sure the base station was still in sight. Getting lost out here was not an option.

Her target sledder was close enough to see each dog clearly. She could pick out their colours and sizes, and hear the steady scrape of the sled's runners knocking across cracks and ridges in the ice crust.

The sled had not slowed, nor changed course, other than to make a few detours around rocky outcrops in the ice. As he came nearer she could see that his face was all but obscured by a fur hood, protection against the cold winds that came with the sled's speed. It could explain why he had apparently not spotted her yet.

She altered course to put herself directly in his path, but as the sled came nearer Ellie began to seriously doubt the sanity of what she was doing. There was no reason to expect him to be hostile, yet she found herself swinging the rifle from her back to rest against her hip, ready and waiting. Being in sight of the camp was all very sensible, but line of sight out here was measured in kilometres. If she got into trouble this far out there was no help. Even if someone back at camp saw her they would not be able to do much.

The sled was pulled not by the usual six or eight dogs but twelve, and as they saw her their noise became deafening. No wonder Apsel's crew were getting so nervous, she thought. She fiddled with the webbing gun strap, and began to measure the distance back. Too late now to change her mind.

Roaring expletives at the dogs in a mixture of Sámi, German and English, the sledder veered slightly to his left, coming between her and the camp; cutting off her escape as he slewed to a halt. He leaned forward from the back of the sled and cracked his whip above the howling canine chaos, separating skirmishes and restoring calm.

Ellie wondered again what in hell she was doing out here, and whether she could get past him without that whip coming in her direction.

He was a big man, towering above the laden sled. She estimated his height at close on two and half metres, far larger than even the local Nordics. He was swathed in traditional Sámi garb rather than contemporary Arctic gear. He turned his attention towards her. There was little of his face to be seen between the furred hood and high collar of his reindeer-hide parka, but she had the impression he was not a young man. Ellie stifled her impulse to whimper like a whipped puppy.

In silence he stepped from the footboard and crunched the gang line's brake hook into the ice, an automatic sequence that spoke of long years behind the runners. He wound the reins across the handlebar, and stomped across the half dozen paces separating him from Ellie, halting just beyond arms reach.

With his whip still clutched in one huge, mitten-cased paw, he pushed his hood back and stared down at her. Ellie realised now he was not just a big man; he was *huge*. A neck-creaking hugeness that forced her to look upwards into cold eyes of slate grey, their whites now coloured a dull, vein-threaded yellow, the skin around them creased and wind-burnt. He pawed at his face mask, pulling it down just far enough to reveal a wide mouth with thin dark lips and startlingly white teeth. Amongst those leathery creases, which covered his whole face, she could not avoid noticing a series of faded white scars. They ran around his jaw line and neck and across his brows.

He wasn't angry as she had expected, or even faintly hostile. Not a fleck of aggression in him – provided she ignored that whip.

'Hi.' She wondered what language he spoke by habit. Her Norwegian was miniscule and her Sámi non-existent. And that wasn't even considering the other possibilities up here like German or Russian or – heaven forbid – the throat-grinding Finnish tongue. She was sure he had used English commands to his dogs; she could only hope the rest of his English was good.

Sometimes hopes exceed expectations. 'Good evening, Miss,' he said. His voice was deep as she had anticipated, but equally soft, which she definitely hadn't. 'Richard Burton' vowels, with the slightest edge; some tiny hint of accent that was out of place here. His English was cultured, yes, but not his native tongue. 'You come from there?' He waved the whip's haft at the camp and she could only nod by way of reply. 'Hmmmm.' The sound he made was not so much a word as a deep rumble of acceptance. His nod was slow, almost a bow. 'You should not be out here alone, Miss. There are bears – and other things.'

Ellie had the impression of amusement in those eyes, though the voice remained politely passive. 'I was told that. I couldn't sleep, though. Then I heard the dogs. And I saw you out here—' She halted, aware she was babbling. Something she never did; cool was her default setting. It was her infallible ability to charm that had got her this far in the trade.

She exhaled, glancing at her ski tips before she raised

her gaze back to his face and held out her hand. 'My name is Ellie Levin. You may have read some of my articles?'

That face was blank, and no name was offered in return, which didn't match up. That voice spoke of manners and elegance. And in Ellie's experience any man with a voice like that would keep to the social niceties.

'Elizabeth,' she said, 'Elizabeth Le—'

'*No!*'

She flinched from his bark, and flinched again as the dogs released a fresh chorus of yips. The sledder stumbled a few paces away and stood motionless for a moment with his back toward her and his head bowed. As if sensing their driver's mood the dogs began to yammer, heads thrown back in sharp, mist-wreathed jerks with each sound.

Ellie grasped the rifle, swinging it to the ready, and wondered for a split moment if her best option wouldn't be to just run.

It was several long seconds before the sledder straightened and turned to face her, rapping out a sharp command to the dogs to hush. The silence that followed was broken by a few tiny whimpers. The sledder advanced the few steps he had given way and she renewed her grip on the gunstock, the barrel snouting toward him unsteadily.

He glanced at it, then reached out to gently turn it away. 'Forgive me,' he murmured. 'You took me by surprise. I had no intention of causing you anguish. I speak so seldom with anyone now. If indeed I ever did speak often.'

She lowered the weapon, embarrassed at her actions. 'Apology accepted. I wanted to talk with you, if that's all right?' She tucked the rifle under her right arm and reached into her pocket for her tiny cam-recorder, holding it up and flicking it to record. 'Do you mind?'

'What does it do?'

'It makes sure that I have what you say exactly right. Nothing to worry about.' She took his lack of reply as an acceptance. It was already running in any case. 'Just speak clearly and naturally. 'I am here in the Arctic researching world myths',' she said into the recorder, smiling at him. 'Following up on recent rumours of the Arctic Sasquatch, or Yeti. And quite by chance I have come across a wanderer of the inland wastes of Finnmark. Land of ice and the midnight sun. Can I ask you sir, have you ever seen things up here that cannot be explained?'

He didn't answer for a moment, regarding her with sad resignation. 'Sasquatch? I have heard nothing of that thing. What is it?'

'Never heard of a Yeti either?'

He shook his head. 'You must forgive my ignorance. I have not been in contact with the civilised world for some time.'

'You must have heard of the Yeti at least? It's basic Crypto-zoology,' she said. 'Creatures of mystery? Monsters to some.'

His dark lips jerked into what was obviously an unfamiliar upward posture, the merest shadow of a smile. 'I have heard of many monsters. I have seen but two.'

'You've seen the monster?' She struggled to maintain

her calm, aware this was probably her only chance at this one. 'Tell me more, please.'

He sighed and walked back to his sled, retrieving his ice brake with a practised flick of his wrist. 'You seek monsters? Look around you. The world exists for them.'

'But you said you had seen two, right here. Can you give me details?'

The sledder laughed sharply and unhitched his reins. 'One died, and I vowed once to burn the other. Hey up, team! Hike! Hike!' He flicked the leather strapping and his lead dog renewed her howling command to her underlings. The team lurched eagerly into their harness.

Ellie jumped back. Already the sled was slipping past.

'Be safe, Elizabeth,' he shouted at her 'There are more kinds of monsters than you can ever capture on a page.' His hand snaked out and whipped the recorder from her.

She had a brief notion of its movement as it arced into the air and then crashed ice ward.

And then he was gone. Vanished, somewhere in the red-gold haze.

She waited, listening for any hint of the singing of dogs or the deep booming of that dark voice. She should have caught some echo. The smallest sounds travelled far beyond normal ranges out here. But there was nothing to be heard except the wind and the creaking thaw; and, eventually, her own shuddering body as immobility permitted cold breezes to penetrate the fabrics of her parka and all that lay beneath to her very heart.

Ellie skittered toward the recorder's last visible point, raggedly, stiff from the chill, but revitalising as her blood ran faster with her physical efforts. A couple of sweeps didn't come up with that precious machine and its unique recording. What had transpired between her and him was lost to all but the two of them. Nothing left to do but head back to the camp, her return slower than her exit.

*

Apsel's dogs didn't bark at her return. Which was puzzling until she noticed Apsel lurking in the lee of the stores shack, rifle cradled across the crook of his left arm.

'Told you not to go out alone,' he said, turning toward their cabin. 'One day you're going to get dead, lady.'

'Probably.' She unlatched her skis and followed him inside, homing in on the coffee.

As she heated water and retrieved mugs she sensed Apsel watching her, waiting for her. Vapour drifting from the kettle spout matched her own head of steam. 'What?' she snapped. 'You got something else to say?'

'Stallo,' he said. 'That's what you saw. That was Stallo.'

'You were watching me? You stood back here and watched?'

He shrugged. 'You're no child. You go out chasing shadows? Your business.'

'But you saw.' She handed him a mug, coming close up to smile into his face in an attempt to appeal to the man in him. 'You can verify the sighting. This would be huge, Apsel. Make you famous.'

'The Big One don't want to know so much. We respect that. While he travels we are good. Safe. They say when the Big One finds his place, when he finds his peace and he burns then the world will end.'

'Who says? I've never heard this legend.'

'Not a legend,' Apsel replied. 'When I was small, my grandma would talk of this. She remembers her mother telling her 'bout when the Big One came a long time ago. He came looking for his maker. She says when the Big One finds him, he'll go to the end of the world to burn. Until then the Big One comes and he goes, and always he travels north. That is the story my grandma told me. We leave him alone. He needs nothing from us. It's what I always said. The Stallo is a Troll.' He turned to walk away. 'You know what that means?' he said from the doorway. 'This Troll?'

'It's a mythical being that...'

'Stallo is Troll.' He vanished from view, only his voice left for a parting shot. 'But Troll in your words is The Monster.'

# Gallery Green

THE GALLERY HAD grabbed the usual bouquet of design awards and sufficient brickbats to start a reasonable sized wall. Karrin thought it was pretty bloody amazing. From the pavement, staring up that blue-black facade, she was certain that, love or hate it, no one standing in its shadow could avoid feeling some kind of awe. That overwhelming sense of mortality, normally reserved for cathedrals and palaces, inspired by a column of steel and apparently seamless glass rising six stories above the street. This was the brand new, and highly controversial, Tate Modern, Bristol, and she knew the world would beat at its doors whatever words passed on either side of that debate.

Above the entrance a rank of feather flags snapped and flapped the exhibition's multi-hued logo to the wind in a brashly sophisticated welcome. Beneath them a chattering crowd of lesser beings was segregated from the Celebs by ubiquitous metal barriers. Less-privileged photographers lacking press passes snapped and whirred their glass eyes as she passed. Spectators, there to gawk at the glitterati in their black-tie designer-splendour, eyed her suspiciously. The more knowing Arties, who were camped out for the following day's public opening, dismissed her as a nothing, a nobody.

She felt uncomfortable being here. This rarefied end of

the Art world always unsettled her. She still felt vaguely fraudulent. Yes, she had a couple of minor local exhibitions to her name, but hardly the Turner Prize. Cameras clicked and flashed, and she could almost hear a few hundred pairs of eyes slashing at her back with two questions. Who is she? And why does she get in so easy? Knowing her invitation was the real deal did not stop her feeling that way; and the security guys, handing back her card with such scepticism, backed that up. She had that certain feeling they waved her through only because the Holographic-Ticket could not lie.

Walking into the building was such a buzz, and she smiled. Russ had always referred to these events and the people in them as the Art-ificials. 'It's not the real world,' he had said so very often. 'It's not art. It's money. It's a sell out. It's a bloody con.' *But that was B.B.*, she thought. *Before Becki.* Now it was all changed, and even he, the great artiste, had plunged both feet into the murky waters of commerciality.

She was so late, so *very* late, and Becki would be furious. *Best opening in years and she'll say I've blown it*, she thought. Her own tiny gallery had been quiet all day, until a couple of browsers sauntered in right before closing. 'Just looking,' they'd said. It had got *so* late she had almost decided not to bother. Once she passed through the Tate's main foyer into the Grand Hall, however, she knew that staying away would have been her biggest mistake. This was everything the promos had promised and more.

Muted lighting reflected off the pale marble floor and walls. Pale metal stanchions supported the six floors, and, ultimately, the infamous cone shaped glass roof that gave the project the subtitle 'Cornetto Tower'.

The ground floor was one vast atrium with a glistening spiral of stairs running up to the top floor. From there the glass ceiling cone poked upward into the night, and from that darkened structure shards of pure colour were apparently hurtling toward her in jagged swathes. She knew this piece – knew the artist, in fact. Russ Willis was an arsehole. A total git of epic degrees. Yet he had conceived this. She stared at the installation, feeling her pride and loss in familiar stabbing twists of the gut. 'Destruction of the Rainbow' was an old friend. She had seen its tiny prototype, and helped in the cutting of its glass sections. It was the *only* thing she had ever seen him working on. His obsession and his reason. Yet still she was unprepared for the real beast.

It was breath taking. The shattered spectrum, carefully edged in finely hammered silver, held in a timeless free-fall, as each piece lazily twirled on gleaming steel chains. Swaying in the updraft, despite their weight, they nudged at each other, whispering and tittering amongst themselves at each new visitor who dared to stare. It diffused the wall lights into a mosaic of shifting patterns on the pale floor. She had stepped into the maelstrom, unwary and unprepared, and she paused, vaguely disconcerted that the floor itself seemed insubstantial, like the rippling surface of a clouded lake.

Her dress of white silk and silver trim was caught in the same dance, as tiny mirrored decals on wrap and dress sparked flashes of colour like tiny lights, so that she felt like some very small, and very pale, Christmas tree caught in a psychedelic vortex. It made her vaguely nauseous.

A movement lower in the spiral caught her attention, a glass lift gliding toward the top level, mirrored by its twin descending on the far side, synchronised like pendulum weights, marking the hours, the minutes, the moments.

She tracked its path avidly, glad for any distraction against the rainbow's glamour. From its destination on the top floor came faint chinking from glasses of a very different kind, along with soft twin hums of music and voices. Unmistakable sounds of 'launch party' were seeping from what the programme condescendingly informed her was the 'Discourse Arena' on the sixth floor.

Karrin crossed the few last metres, stepped into the waiting lift, and came out at eye level with the shattered Rainbow. She made a deliberate effort not to see it, but to look through it to the other side, in anticipation of the art and the artists she could rub shoulders with. He would not get in her way tonight, not even by proxy.

She searched the crowd for Becki, Chief Curator and her oldest friend. There had been a time, of late, when they had not been friends. There had been a time, not very long ago, when they had been close to killing each other. Over a man, of course. When best-girl-friends stopped talking it's always over a man. But best-girl-friends are friends forever, and once that fanny-rat had cleared the scene they were back to guzzling wine, and giggling, and comparing tales of his chipolata-prick, and his terminal halitosis.

Karrin glanced at the Rainbow and sighed. She should be over it all by now. Art was art, to be appreciated whoever gave it life. What else was there? 'Forget him.

Bastard little toad,' she muttered.

Becki was waving to her, and had left a bevy of art's finest maestros and divas and ingénues to join her at the glass and steel balustrade. She slid her arm beneath Karrin's to link them together as they stared for a moment at the Rainbow.

'Is he here?' Karrin whispered, finally.

Becki laughed quietly. 'Are you really asking me that?'

'I guess not. He's got star billing.'

'Karrin – understand. The Rainbow was already commissioned. And even if it wasn't – it is special. Enjoy it for what it is. As Art. Then move on. But enough of him. What kept you? I was beginning to think you'd bailed. Cold feet again?'

Moving away from the barrier, with arms if not mind still linked with her mentor, Karrin forced herself into calm. Becki often avoided answering merely by ignoring the question, an arrogance that she, Karrin, had to ignore in turn. 'I know Becki. I was so held up in the shop, a couple of time wasters who would not take the hint.'

'Should have shut up shop early. God, Karrin. This is a chance for you to get out of that bloody back alley of yours and make your name.'

'I can't just close. You should know that. And not so much of the back alley,' She grinned and hugged Becki's arm. 'I'm making a nice profit this quarter, thanks to the last two artists you sent me. Best shows I've had. Thanks. I really will owe you.'

'Course you will.' Becki grinned tugged her toward the throng, her arm still looped with Karrin's in a gesture of sisterhood for all to see. 'You do know I'll collect. No matter. You're here now. Come and meet Benny. He's setting up a new exhibition that I think you two could really connect. I'll set you going then it's down to you. Circulate darling. Get your face under the right noses.'

Not advice Karrin could afford to ignore. She circulated herself to a standstill and then drifted to the bar for a fresh glass to ease the next round, hugging her Blackberry to her breast like a baby. More names and contacts had gone in it tonight than she'd collected in years of slogging round the circuit on her own. Becki had really come up with the goods. *She is so going to own me.* Awash with so many names and faces, and so much red wine, she was more than happy to park herself in a quiet corner whilst her friend did her 'thing' with the departing guests.

She took a fresh glass and wandered off to view one of the halls that she had not had time for yet. The party had circulated in sections covering the big Names and of course the Installations that the press always loved so much. She wanted to see the Outsider Gallery. *It's one bit I have an 'outside' chance of ever being exhibited in. And I need to walk off this damn wine. I need a clear head. If I get half the things I've been promised tonight, I'll be in there damn soon,* she told herself.

She glanced at her watch. Almost one a.m. Surely Becki and her staff had kicked out the last few by now?

The two women had arranged a late supper. *But at this rate it could turn out to be an early breakfast.* She sipped the last of her wine and pulled a face, realising she had been clutching the glass by the bowl and turned it from room temperature to blood heat. It hit her stomach, acid and unrelenting, to join the rest of the evening's quota.

*Not good on an empty gut.* She rubbed at her forehead and tried to focus on her surroundings. She had come full circle back to the top floor now and stepped out of the lift as she had at the start of the evening.

The rainbow shards claimed her attention yet again, glittering now with eerie intensity under dimming lights. She could hear Becki's strident tones wafting up from the atrium floor. Looking over the balcony Karrin glimpsed the last few guests being ushered toward the exit.

With their going a quiet settled and only the rainbow was left whispering in soft tinks and chinks as thick chunks of coloured glass collided in slow motion. The sound was mesmerising, doubly so in her wine induced haze, and she watched the sheets of silicate swaying for some moments without any real thoughts running through her mind. Swallowing the last of the wine in her glass regained her attention. She grimaced and ran her tongue around her front teeth to push off the gritty lees that lingered there. *Becki needs to speak with her caterers,* she thought. *The wine waiters are crap.*

Across the space, through the glass forest, a movement caught her attention. The lift had opened and someone stepped out. 'Becki?' she called. 'Can we eat now?'

The half obscured outline paused – looked at her – turned away. She recognised it – him. 'Russell-fucking-Willis. What the hell is he doing here now?'

*Rhetorical question,* she thought. *Of course he's bloody here. He's one of Becki's star turns.* She stared at him through the evidence of his stardom, twisting and turning between them. He was staring straight back, his familiar face framed momentarily in a wafting section of green, pitted glass. It distorted his features, throwing his image toward her as a rippling gargoyle. She shuddered, gripping the rail in front of her; fighting off the panic that numbed her legs and fingers and face.

Six floors below Becki was crossing the floor, her heels clipping on marble sharp and clear, pausing directly under her now, on the edges of vision waiting for the upward car. Across the void the far lift was preparing for descent.

'Russ? What are you doing here? Hey!' Karrin ran around the gallery barrier, and called out to him again. 'Russ?'

She could see him, smiling at her. Waiting. Watching. A few paces more and she would reach him. She stopped some three metres short. 'Have you been here all evening?' she said. 'I didn't see you'

'I've been here all night, Kara mia, and I've seen you.'

'Oh.' She was thankful at being too shocked to blush. The idea of him watching her was creepy, which helped her raise some rapid defences. Before today she had always relapsed into the gauche student in his presence, eager for her Master's approval. But after a year of bitterness and a lot of very expensive therapy— He was just a really creepy guy. She was an artist. She ran a successful business. She was her own person now. 'Really?' she said. 'You surprise me, though I wasn't really looking.' That tautness around his lips was heartening. *A hit*. She thought. *Go on you slimy bastard. Say something else. I'm ready*. 'Glad you made it,' she added. 'Glad you've arrived in fact. Nice to know someone else from our class is actually making a living the way they intended. From their art.'

'Oh, I'm here,' he said. 'Always will be.' He nodded at the Rainbow. 'Immortality. It's what we're all after. Right?'

'Depends on how you go about it. So, you and Becki. She says you're not together now.'

'No need.' He nodded again at his glass memorial.

Glancing at the shards Karrin had to smile. All that angst and jealousy, wondering what Becki had that she didn't. *And really*? she thought. *It's nothing. He's a user. A lying, cheating snivel-nosed loser.* 'So, good for you,' she said. 'What next? More rainbows?'

'No. Once the statement is made, once it's out there, anything else can only be a reflection.' He grasped the balustrade and looked down. 'I have one final statement though. And I wanted you to be the messenger.' He took a last look at her, and waving his fingers in mocking farewell, swung up onto a seat running along the side and stepped out into the air.

Watching him fall wasn't like slow motion. Not as such. But she would play those few seconds on constant repeat, so that it did get to feel that way.

His hair lifted, his shoulders hunched in that odd way that they always did when he walked. One leg, then the other, arms bent and out, almost as if he were steadying himself for his descent. Almost as if he intended to catch the updraft and fly up and out of the atrium and become a part of his precious Rainbow.

What he did was plummet. She turned away, stomach boiling and imagined falling with him. She did not see, but she heard him hit the ground, and his body made a curiously musical, bell-like sound. Loud, deafening, and then the black cloud came down in a high-pitched hum, as though she was enveloped in an impenetrable, cloying, swarm of insects that wrapped around her head, as dense as velvet and cold as glass. She knew there were other sounds, voices, some close and some away off down that long black tunnel. Karrin hung in stasis, vivid glimpses of colour whisking past her in blurred gyrations. In her memory the Rainbow was forming, bursting, and reforming, over and over in kaleidoscopic tumult.

Then Becki was beside her trying to pull her hands together, and shouting at her to,

'Stop screaming and listen'.

'I have to get down there. He needs help,' Karrin leaned back, struggling weakly at the hands clasping around her own.

'I imagine he's beyond help,' said Becki. 'Wait with me, Karrin. Security has everything under control. The Police will want to speak with you I think.'

'Police? He needs ambulances, paramedics.'

'The Police will be here for you, not him.'

'What?'

'I saw, Karrin. I saw what happened.'

'But…'

'I saw what you did. I never imagined you would react that way.'

She seemed sincere. To all intents and purposes Becki was the concerned friend calming and reassuring. On the surface she was all that Karrin could want under duress, yet she had the definite feeling there was more than appearances would hint. 'Saw?' she whispered.

'You were arguing,' Becki said. 'Don't you remember? And then you tried to lift him up, he fell.'

'No. No, that wasn't the way. He climbed up.'

'I saw, Karrin.'

It was not true. Karrin knew it. Becki had not seen her do anything, she couldn't have seen it. She couldn't have. 'I need to see,' she moaned, and ran to the stairs. Becki did not attempt to stop her.

At ground level she stopped to look at the remnants. Crimson smears ran through the gyrating swirls, marking the place where Russ had fallen. In the centre of the smears lay a cream coloured blanket; rumpled and blood soaked.

Karrin stepped forward. People were talking to her. She ignored them. They were distant, far and far away, and without words. She did not understand or need to listen to them. They were nothing. Droning insects returned to keep the people away. High and insistent, breaking through to the centre of her skull and messing with her senses.

A few steps closer, and she could see smears of blood all around her. Spatters had streaked the closer stanchions and gouts of scarlet gloop were pooled nearest to the blanket in thick, viscous lumps – looking more like jammy rice than blood spill. She swallowed hard and forced her bile back down her throat. Yet she could not help herself from staring.

Someone was next to her, holding her arm. Becki.

'Where has he gone?' Karrin turned dull eyes toward her oldest friend. 'Where?'

'Probably the ambulance guys already scraped him up,' Becki replied. 'The little cockroach was still breathing when I got to him. It wasn't for long. He's dead, Karrin.'

'Poor Russ. I never thought he'd do anything like that.'

'I saw, Karrin. I read all those emails you sent him so I know you wanted him dead. No one will blame you. I can't blame you. Me least of all.'

'No. He jumped.'

'Karrin. I saw,' Becki replied. 'I saw what you did.'

'So the Police are here? It's not fair Becki. I never did it. Believe me. I never killed him. You have to know that. Please Becki. Help me. Please.'

Becki glanced around her. 'Let's get you somewhere safe, shall we? Then we can think.'

The familiar face before her was wavering, the voice distant, and through it there was something Karrin felt she should be doing, had to be doing. Something she should be saying to someone about something. 'Me?' she mumbled. 'What happened?'

'I saw,' Becki said. 'But they don't have to know, do they?'

\*

Nothing works like bad publicity to make yourself a name in art. From here in her own rooms she could earn a mint. Not that she would ever get to spend that much of it. There was little to spend it on in a private and very *secure* nursing home. She could paint all she wanted, and sell almost everything, and no one ever knew what she did. What Becki said she did.

*She has to be right*, Karrin thought. *If I could remember, then it would all be good. Maybe I could get out of here. If only I could see what went before that bloody blanket. If I painted a Camera obscura, seeing what went before.*

Her subject matter seldom changed. Rainbows over

red boiling sunsets. Rainbows over deep grey seas. Rainbows over cemeteries and rooftops. Time and again she re-assembled those images from her black tunnel, searching for that memory and always failing. It was gone, lost over the rainbow. Somewhere she would never find it. Not in this life.

She even painted him, occasionally. She didn't need to try remembering his face, because he came to see her ... when no one was there. Mostly he came to peer through the window, smiling that crooked smile, and mouthing words she could never quite hear. Sometimes he followed Becki when she came to visit and stood behind her; watching and grinning.

'He's there Becki. I tell the doctors, but they won't believe me and now nor do you.'

'No, of course not. Why would we?' Becki patted Russ's arm. 'He's dead, after all. Aren't you dear? I know, because I saw. I saw what you did.'

# City Canal

Still birds swim over the rainbow
That will fade with passing time
Bruised depths moving slow
The banks are high, the water low
Oiling slick turned bathtub rime
Still birds swim over the rainbow
Longboats passing to and fro
Cutting through the surface slime
Bruised depths moving slow

Sunday strolling on the tow
Trying to see beyond the grime
Still birds swim over the rainbow
Abandoned car, discarded barrow
Surreptitious acts of crime
Bruised depths moving slow
Green canal now wreathed in sorrow
Unwanted, wasted past its prime
Still birds swim over the rainbow

Bruised depths moving slow

# Thirteenth Day

*The King sent his Lady on the Thirteenth day*
*Three stalks of corn.*
*Two maids a-merry dancing.*
*Three hinds a-merry dancing*
*An Arabian baboon.*
*Three swans a-merry swimming*
*Three ducks a-merry laying.*
*A bull that was brown.*
*Three gold spinks*
*Three starlings*
*A goose that was grey.*
*Three plovers*
*Two partridges, and a papingo-aye.*
*Who learns my carol and carries it away.*

(Old Scottish carol to tune
'Twelve Days of Christmas')

'THE SECOND DAY,' said the Holly-Man. He was rugged. Fragile. A woodsman in a shabby green duster and heavy boots. Behind him stood a boy in an Acorn-hat, waiting in silence.

Kat tweaked a tight smile and went on hacking at the ice-bound soil, hoping they would take a hint and leave. They didn't.

With a flourish, The Holly-Man offered his hat, its iridescent starling-feather brim, and holly-sprigged band oddly vivid. 'My favour to you, dear lady.'

Stabbing her fork into the hard soil she squared up to him. 'If you're collecting for the church I've no change on me.'

Uphill, toward the wood, a horn sounded. Kat turned to see a single rider on a white horse disturbing a pair of partridges from the heather before melting into the trees,

When she looked back the strangers were gone. 'Weirdo'. Kat continued her assault on frozen parsnips until screeching from the barn reminded her late aunt's bequest of cottage and land had included a small menagerie. Three ducks, two goats, one evil tempered goose and, for some obscure reason, a particularly savage peacock, all of which needed tending before dark

She went to bed that night exhausted, her dreams permeated by dark and beautiful terrors.

*

When she woke a spiked unease drove her into the village, not only for supplies but to rub shoulders with humanity and slough away her jitters.

Kat was returning with her few purchases when she noted the ornate bird cage perched on the front step. Three goldfinches fluttered against the bars, panicking at her proximity. On impulse she bent, and flicked the cage open, and watched them flit toward the woodland.

Another gift. Was someone stalking her? Should she report it? What could she say? That she, a newcomer, who knew no one, was receiving gifts from unseen neighbours? As crimes went it was unlikely to bring the constabulary running. She sighed. It was late and there was stock to feed. Tomorrow she would go back to the village to ask around.

*

Another morning and unease sent Kat to the village to see who might be able to identify her visitor, and returned at dusk, none the wiser.

She almost stepped on a package left squarely on the doormat. Picking it up she scanned the surrounding garden and open hillside. There was nobody in sight. Kat took the parcel inside to unwrap its folds of blue gauze. Whatever she expected it was not this small bronze bull.

She acknowledged a certain frisson at these unexpected gifts, but placed the bull outside and bolted the door against its cold stare.

*

It snowed all night, and all of the next day and night. Her thoughts skirled, dwelling on her predicament, cut off from civilisation. She drifted often to the doors, always anticipating a gift. She was often disappointed.

Finally, there on the step, propped back to back, was a pair of Christmas tree fairies; glittering and perfect.

She scooped them up eagerly, turning them this way and that, looking for something to identity what they could mean. They represented something familiar, that she should know well enough, but what?

*

After another dream-wrecked night she could barely summon the energy for surprise at a squat stone ape on her garden path. She eyed it warily, careful to avoid contact, and careful to lock the door against her stalkers once her chores were done.

It was close to midnight when her imprisonment

finally got to her and she ventured out into the eeriness of a snow-lit garden. After the stuffy confines of the cottage the breeze smelled of snow, crisp, almost spicy. Her footfalls possessed that deadened quality, where sound froze a single pace from origin. Yet others carried sharp into the silence. Bells, for example, and the chinking of harness, or snow-deadened clumping of horses' hooves.

Hunters, horses and hounds, emerged from the wood, their outlines blurred and shifting and indistinct. Kat held her breath, drawing into the cover of the apple trees to watch. The lead rider signalled a halt, whirling her mount around to face her followers.

Behind her rode the Holly-hatted Man, and beside him the Acorn-hatted Boy who shouted excitedly, pointing across the fields. The hunt took off after three fat hinds and within a few moments had moved out of sight.

*

By morning snow that last night had resembled a ploughed field was table top smooth.

In Aberdeenshire, being snowed in with communications cut to nil lacked novelty, but when the door bell chimed she jumped. Who could reach her here? She wrestled the door free of its latest drift, and found a silver medallion looped from the porch eaves. She tugged it free to examine it. The ornate silver tracery depicted three enamelled swans and three tiny corn sheaves.

She almost dropped it at the sudden noise in the lane – A horse sidling impatiently in the snow, its rider, swathed in a fur-lined cape, oblivious to driving winds that blew her hood back and revealed her silver hair.

'When you learn our song take care not to be carried on its dream,' the woman called. 'The days grow longer, and that will not change.' She smiled sadly. 'Many others have been drawn into the Wheel before you – and failed. Your aunt knew all this and did her duty well and was well rewarded. I offer you the same protection, and a word of advice. Keep you to your hearth this night.' She kicked her heels and her mount lurched into a loping stride through a gap in the hedge and away toward the hill.

Kat went to retreat indoors, but there, tucked into her Christmas wreath, was the cap she had first seen in the hands of Holly-man. Plainly the Lady had not left it, her warnings against involvement had been very clear, but this could be the reason for the warning. She plucked the hat down and smoothed its feathered brim, glancing curiously after her visitor.

On the rise two riders looked on, and she did not need them any closer to know them. As the Lady passed them the younger man turned to follow, but the other lingered, staring down at Kat. His horse started a few tentative steps downhill when the Lady stopped on the edge of the trees and called out. Holly-man looked down at the cottage one last time before he too followed her into the wood.

Glancing down at the brooch in one hand and cap in the other Kat wondered what madness had decided her to spend the festive season here alone. She slammed the door and fumbled the chain across with trembling hands, and, leaning her back against its solidity, wrapped her arms around herself.

Her aunt had held some odd views. Eccentric, mad some said, fixated on times past. Kat dredged her memory for anything that could fit all of this.

She had gained a favour and a warning in one day. What was it she was supposed to know? Was she expected to take sides? With no idea what was at stake, for her or anyone else how could she possibly know? Tonight was obviously the denouement for whatever, and she was fairly certain locking herself indoors would be no protection from whatever it would entail.

*

That night was calm. Its clear sky plunged temperatures low enough to freeze the snow into meringue-crust mounds and troughs that almost took Kat's weight as she ploughed her way across to a vantage point at the edge of her property. She had not long to wait before the hunt appeared.

The Lady led them onto the white arena, but tonight hunting was clearly not their game. Riders and hounds alike spread out into a wide circle, facing inward and waiting, silent, patient.

The Lady stared toward Kat for a long moment and raised a hand briefly, palm out; her only acknowledgement of Kat's presence.

The meaning was clear. Kat could hear the warnings the Lady had given earlier chiming clear in her head.

The Lady turned to raise her hand again, this time to gather her troop's attention.

Kat looked on, hardly breathing.

The Holly-Man and Acorn-Boy had dismounted now and waded through the snow to the centre of the arena. Each carried a broadsword that glinted silver-moonlight in their hands.

They bowed first to their Lady and then to each other.

The Holly-man gazed toward Kat.

She stretched out her arms, with palms up in an exaggerated shrug; there was nothing she could do.

The Lady nodded toward her, and barked out a command that Kat did not quite catch, but understood emphatically.

Holly-man shrank a little, defeated in that moment though whether by the order or by Kat's gesture she would never know.

The two men began trading blows in curiously sedate fashion until Holly-Man halted.

He looked toward Kat and raised his sword.

He kissed it.

Bowed to Kat and to his opponent and to his Lady.

He knelt, with head bowed, resting on the sword hilt with blade buried deep though the snow into the sleeping turf beneath.

His adversary's two-handed blow took him full in the neck.

Kat closed her eyes, steadying against the blood-horror echoing in her skull. This was no fight. This was an execution.

She opened her eyes.

The hillside was pristine.

# Green Tea

THEY TRAVELLED IN silence. Niki because she was so very angry, Fliss because she had yet to consume her regulation half bucket of coffee.

Niki hated how her twin practised the dumb blonde image. The one she had been cultivating since they were kids, though she was as natural a brunette as Niki. Hair and eyes were the external similarities taken as read for identical twins which no amount of hair dye and coloured contacts could ultimately change. It was their inner differences that surprised many. They perceived twins to be inseparable; to think and live as one. 'They' were wrong.

Niki had flown the cage straight from school and headed for the Holistic Medicine School at Aberdeen, Fliss had opted for the far more acceptable Art History doctorate and lived at home.

Niki's empathy as a therapist was legendary to clients but for her twin, in fact for all of her family, it was in astoundingly short supply. Fliss had never given a damn. When Niki offered to help Fliss get over the shock of their parent's sudden death it had been a massive gesture. Six months down the line Fliss showed no sign of returning to London, or finding herself a job.

The gestures Niki offered to this lassitude were of a particularly biological nature. She decided Fliss was going to earn her keep and set her to work at Cabin Therapy, one of the Tissingford Craft Centre's features housed in its two dozen log cabin styled units. Reassuringly rustic, yet glittery new in a shining steam-treated polished golden yellow way. It was her steam-treated holistic haven.

Niki sighed as she pulled on the handbrake. She prided herself on her work ethic and being first in last out. And having her record impugned by her own sister was just the end. If nothing else she could set Fliss on the right track and re-educate her twin for the 21st century. Years of their parent's toxic consumerism was something Niki was resolved to deal with in her twin. She could at least show her where their mother had gone wrong.

'You can help on the front desk again today.' Niki knew her voice sounded artificial, over bright, full of hastily gathered bonhomie. 'I know it's not your thing, but you can at least answer the phones. And try not to taunt the clients like you did last week.'

Fliss stood peering about her sulkily. 'I can work at being a tree hugger,' she said. 'Just try me.' She picked a flake of nail polish from her cuticle, held her right hand up with slender fingers splayed into a curved fan to admire her handiwork, and then gifted her twin with a sly wink. 'If there's money it.'

'You've already got free board and lodgings. If things work out this week then we'll talk about pay.' Niki shoved her toward the backroom. 'Now go and put on something more suitable than those god-awful sweats.'

Twenty minutes later Fliss reappeared, clad in a simple white tunic and trousers. From somewhere she had scrounged make-up and a hairdryer and she looked fabulous, which irritated the hell out of Niki.

'Drink this.' She thrust a mug into Fliss's hands.

'What is it?' Fliss peered at the pale, bluish, liquid inside. 'Oh, God. Not one of you crappy fruit teas?'

'Green tea with elderberry.' Niki flapped a hand encouragingly. 'Drink it. Heaps of antioxidants.'

'It smells rank.'

'Stop whining and drink. Far better for you than a caffeine fix.'

'Do I care? I just want my coffee.'

'You'll care in ten years time when your arteries and liver have hardened and your joints are crumbling. You'll care.'

Fliss sipped at the tea, shuddered and poured it down the sink the moment her twin's back was turned.

Niki would have been annoyed at the waste, the ingratitude, the arrogance, had the shop not jingled away her attention. She was already on the move, out into the bright foyer full of comfy leather sofas, coffee tables and discreet carousels of leaflets, incense and malas. She was smiling, and serene, and waiting patiently for the two women drifting around the foyer to get close enough for the sales pitch.

Twenty-five minutes later she was back in the staff room, her natural tranquillity buoyed up by the sale of one half day pamper package, a full body massage and two shiatsu consults.

'Good start to the day,' she flicked on the kettle and whisked a teabag into her favourite mug. 'I'll need to ring Tina and Lauren to help out. They'll be pleased with an extra shift. It's been quiet this past month.' Niki paused, wrinkling her nose at the harsh taint of coffee pervading the tiny space.

Fliss wafted her Starbucks in her sister's general direction; Niki spritzed the air with lemon grass and lavender to eliminate all trace of caffeine.

Taking out a tissue to wipe the descending mist from the plastic lid of her cup, Fliss slurped noisily from her double shot grande. Niki retreated, her tea unmade and her newly risen mood melting fast.

Fliss had a knack of puncturing her serenity bubble; just as their mother had always done. All her sister had done was offer Niki a sip of coffee. In so many eyes that was a 'nice' gesture, an olive branch given how they had begun their day together.

Niki knew better. It was a depth charge. A calculated swipe at everything she held dear. A poison, delivered in that sweet and helpless, bubble-brained blonde way that Fliss used, wearing her platinum crop like the roman charioteer's helmet it closely resembled; brash and impenetrable.

'She has got to go.'

'Pardon? Did you say something?'

Niki turned toward the voice, flushing slightly. She hadn't realised anybody was in the shop. 'I'm sorry. I was thinking aloud. Can I help you at all?'

'I was just looking for Felicity.'

He was tall and fair, clean shaven and even featured. Not bad to look at, but not memorable. Except for the voice, which was deeper than his looks would lead a girl to believe possible from such a slight frame. Niki thought him attractive, the kind of guy she went for. But he seemed vaguely familiar among the many men that accompanied her largely female clientele. A man like that, she had thought, is bound to belong to somebody. 'Does she know you?' She asked.

'Yes. Not, well, granted. Only met her here yesterday. She's an interesting woman. Colin.' He held out his hand. 'Colin Read. You must be Nicole?'

That figured. He would be looking for 'Felicity'. She could never be 'Fliss' to a walking wallet. Niki forced a smile. 'I will go and get her for you.'

'Would you? That's awfully kind.'

Niki didn't want to see that smile again. They were identicals, yet Fliss somehow mastered her image in a way Niki had never managed, and used it to lasso man after man with nauseating ease. 'Fliss? Someone asking for you.'

Neither of them said a word. The animosity on one side and triumph on the other was a set given; their natural state of interaction since walking and talking had erupted into their first battle. They only passed in the doorway, sidling, breathing to avoid even their clothes from touching. Fliss's cut-crystal giggle from the shop front grated on Niki's roughened sensibilities and she closed her office door.

As she headed for the tranquillity of her consulting room just ten minutes later one of her staff sat at the reception desk. There was no sign of either Fliss or Colin.

'Damn it.' Niki had people to see, and she wasn't feeling so bright today. She did not need Fliss playing hookey like some errant schoolchild. She rubbed at her stomach and suppressed a belch. She was sure it was an ulcer brewing and small wonder with the Cabin to run and the Felicity factor on top of it all.

'Calm,' she told herself. 'Be calm. Stress is my enemy.'

In the months that passed Fliss lived the high life by night and charmed clients by day. Niki bottled her anger and exasperation, and swallowed every stomach acid cure she could lay hands on.

Niki had almost got used to having her twin around – Fliss took an interest in herbals and spa treatments.

After the first flashes of war an uneasy truce there were days when they almost liked each other. Fliss took charge on occasion, waiting on Niki hand and foot as the ulcers made their presence felt over the months. 'You should see a doctor,' Fliss insisted.

'I am a doctor,' Niki replied. 'I just need to rest.'

'Well stay home for a few more days. I can cope.'

'Really?'

'Of course. You just put your feet up. Here,' she handed Niki a cup of hot tea. 'Elderberry. Your favourite.'

'Is this your new recipe?'

Fliss nodded. 'By my own fair hand.'

'Oh. So I'm guinea pig tonight.' She took a large sip. 'Needs honey.'

'Thought it might.' Fliss spooned a dollop into the cup and stirred. 'Better?'

'Thank you. It's heaven. So what did you do with my grotty sister?'

Fliss smiled. 'Just made her useful. Anything else you need? I'm off out shortly.'

'With Colin?' She hadn't meant to sound sharp, but the mention of Fliss's boyfriend always roused the worst in her. Niki reached out to touch Fliss's arm. 'Sorry. Go and have a good time. Make sure you have your key. I'm for a hot bath and bed.'

'I won't be late.' Fliss smiled. 'Can't be out late tonight.'

'Why not?'

'It's a special night. Third time lucky.'

Niki slept, and woke several hours later. Her mind was spinning a little but she felt good, better than she had for days. Maybe she could even go out for a while? Walk to the pub perhaps. Not that she knew too many locals. Work had always come before her social life, but she felt a need to be out and doing. She sat up, and then the pain began. She leaned forward and leaned both hands against the coffee table, head bowed and winced against a grinding spasms in her gut that quite literally snatched her breath away. She sat back again, shocked and gasping against the onslaught. Not so good after all.

She wrapped herself in the woollen throw. Chills and sweats shuddered through her in waves, keeping in time with the spiralling pain and nausea. She closed her eyes, hating the way the room had begun to shimmer around her. And the pain; it was as though a dough hook gathered her gut and pulled it away from her, winding and stretching and knotting each centimetre into an absolute purgatory. She willed herself into calm, drawing on every scrap of meditational technique to push agony back into the recesses. She needed help, but patting her pockets for her mobile drew a blank. Her pulse was banging through her skull at stroke levels now.

Niki inched a painful passage to the far end of the sofa and grabbed for house phone. Lacking co-ordination she knocked it to the floor. She fell after it, flailing her hands in the general direction of the handset. She finally brought it to her ear and listened to a silence broken only by the sounds of her own breathing that was the harsh, all consuming, panting of a rabid hound.

A new deluge of nerve ripping pain, and she paused, hoping the spasms would pass. From somewhere far away down a corridor of hazy, jellified consciousness she heard voices, and laughter. She opened her mouth to call out but only managed a gush of acid, steaming vomit. Inside she was screaming for help, outside she was only screaming; a long wild shrieking crescendo that went on and on and on.

Hands hauled her to the sofa; held her firmly in place as she retched over and over again until she was sure her twisted guts were trying to fling themselves up her gullet and out of her burning mouth. She prised open her eyes at an urgent voice calling her name. Fliss's face, her own face it seemed, was looming through the mists at her. The pain was ebbing, the voices becoming quieter, the face before her fading in and out. 'What?' she whispered. 'What?'

Fliss leaned down to whisper close to her ear. 'Elderberries. And E. Both on the cyanide table. Such a shame that you overdosed. You should have known better. I shall be devastated.'

'Wah? I … no.'

'Oh but you did, sister dear. So sad to end it that way. Everyone always thought you were the strong one.'

Niki shook her head. The pain passed as the world eased into eternal dreamtime.

# The Abused and Him

'GOD IT'S COLD.' She pulls her dressing gown closer. Listening. Tensing at each sound, knowing He is in the house, waiting.

Maybe she'll strike lucky; perhaps tonight is the night He will relent. She shifts position. Her left elbow cracks against the rear wall and she turns to give the painted bricks closer scrutiny, anything to take her mind off of Him. Magnolia. No imagination, some people. Always magnolia, and in this light it's as dingier and more depressing than usual. She looks up at a single naked bulb above her head. One pendulous drop of light.

Shivering again, but not from the cold. Please God, not tonight. Not again. She sinks further down the washroom wall. Her right elbow smacks into the panel partition. Six stone, and even she has a job fitting in here. She knows every knothole in these damned oak panels. Oak? Ha! Someone had delusions of grandeur. Stained pine so thin it buckles if she leans too hard.

She wants to stretch but if she unfurls her legs against the door it will put her feet beyond the comforting tepid warmth of her candlewick gown, exposing them to temperatures rapidly approaching zero. She wonders what the time is. Twelve? One a.m.? Her parents are out a long time tonight. Third night in a row she's sat here, guilty and afraid; and so many nights before that, for how many years? She doesn't like to count them. A lifetime. Not the one she had as a small child, but the one that began with His violations, just a week into her ninth year.

A creak. A scuffle. Goose bumps rise so hard and so numerous her arms feel like lychees. She rubs at her skin to flatten them. She knows that sound. Any second now He will slime down the corridor to assault her senses – and her body.

There, creaking treads where the staircase turns. No-one could ever step over all of them without grabbing the newel post, which creaks more than the treads.

Silence. She relaxes a little. Tonight could be one of the good nights when she will escape. Maybe.

She has to get some warmth to her toes. If they seize now then how can she run away? Looking around, she laughs quietly. Run? Where? He will block her escape through the door. The only other way out of this hole is the window. Eight inches by ten, and a twenty-foot drop straight onto concrete. Broken leg at the very least. More probably her neck.

Is it so wise to hide in here? She will be found. No doubt on that. He knows she'll always be here. It is the only internal door in the house with a lock. A decrepit rim lock of the skimpier variety with fixing screws missing, or half out. One good kick and it will come straight off. Still she twists the key to make sure it's locked.

Why doesn't Mum come back. What if she and Dad don't come back? Does it matter? They don't listen. Mother blames her, punishes her for telling evil lies about her first born son; has closed her eyes to the things going on before her.

Who else can she tell? No-one listens. No-one wants to know, and no-one stops Him coming to her in the night. Her eyes close as a shudder squeezes at her shoulders and ribs. She clamps her teeth together so hard her jaws ache, but it's worth it to stop the sound escaping her lips. Lips quivering. She will not cry. Not again. Tears do not stop Him. Nothing does.

It's her imagination. They said. Nightmares. They said. Or lies from a trouble-making little slut with an evil mind. But it isn't her. He will not leave her alone. Yet in their eyes he can do no wrong. The eldest son. Apple of their eyes.

She scowls. It always seems worse in the dark. The dark makes Him bigger, all of Him. Not just...

Gluing her teeth even tighter, until they might shatter, she tries to think of something else. It's too gross to contemplate.

She can see stars through the window. Tiny bubbles jiggling in unseen traps, struggling to break free from their own prisons. Bright then dim, pulsing out SOSs to someone. Anyone that would help out. A shooting star, slicing black velvet heavens in triumphant escape. She looks away and snorts disgust at herself, getting all poetic about a few stupid stars. She should know better.

Wood brushing carpet: a door cautiously opened? Please no. One creak. A second. A third. They have to get back soon. Hollywood can't be the only place where the cavalry comes to the rescue?

Scuffle, sniff. A staccato whine that isn't Him but herself, jamming a scream into reverse and forcing it down a rigid throat.

*Please God. Not tonight. Give me a break. Prayers do nothing. Nothing does nothing.*

Scuff, cough. Her feet brace the door. Her vision wraps around the door knob, oblivious of the iron cistern pipe pulverising her back bone. *Praise the lord this is such a little space.* Small suddenly seems very beautiful. The knob is turning, shaking; it's so loose, it'll break. A muttered something. She can't be sure what He says, but she knows it won't be any sort of compliment. Threats. Violence. It's all he can give her – has ever given her.

Her pulse resounds through her skull, blots out all other sounds. Mumble. Mutter. Obscenities half uttered, not for her ears, yet they are, and she can feel her legs jellifying.

Silence.

Listen.

Don't breathe.

No sound or she might miss something.

Slithering.

Hammering on the door.

Heavy breathing.

Fingers whitening on the sill above her as the fanlight above the door flips open an inch or two. Eyes stare down at her through the gap. Blue/grey. Staring eyes alight with anger.

Thump of feet hitting the floor.

The door shakes.

The handle has to give, the door collapse, if not from Him shoving inward, then from her forcing it out – splintering wood into long jagged shards.

Sweating under the strain, her skin crawls damp.

A naked fear of naked flesh.

She screams. Fear, anger; and a black shame that is not hers to feel, yet is felt at every waking hour and through her troubled dreams.

Silence.

All gone.

No wood wall. No eyes. No cause.

Alone.

Relief.

The wetness between her shoulders is the same cold sweat. Fear remains a constant, no matter what the time or place.

She pretends to settle, except that her eyes are wide open. She tells herself it was a long time ago, that she's a big girl now; but the memories have never faded. Though He died almost thirty years ago, the knowledge of His existence has burned indelible scars through her dreams. She can barely recall a time before them.

Remembering His death brings a smile to her lips. A slight smile masked in shadows. It isn't always the good who die young. Sometimes fate takes a hand – to keep the balance.

Her eyes close and she is drifting back toward sleep. Dead is forever. He can't return…

Yet he does, often, when the darkness is complete.

# Damnation Seize My Soul

MERCEDEYS BENKS STEPPED out of the main airlock, keeping her back to the wall whilst she surveyed the concourse. After 'crowded', the first word that came to mind was 'dirty'. Though dirt hardly described the layer of engine grease and soot, acquired over many decades, that gave T'uga its distinctive hue and odour. Filth, she thought, was a more embracing term. But if she called any landmass in this universe home then it was this one: T'uga, the sole construct on a barren clod of craters and rifts. Surrounded by a handful of makeshift airlock tunnels, it resembled nothing more than a bloated tic, as did many of the creatures that scurried within it. Few returned there without great need.

Queen Victoria's Admiralty had known it as *HMS Resistance*, once-along-awhile; for a ship it had been, and the largest Dreadnaught ever launched. So large that, away from the witches and mediums of Earth, those who had stolen her could never hope to produce enough ectoplasm to sideslip the mighty steam engines. Running her aground would have been their only viable option.

The concourse was more crowded than she would expect so early in the day. Mercy had often seen T'uga's denizens in turmoil, yet seldom so determinedly space-bound as today. They toted duffel-bags and banded trunks and an obvious urgency to be somewhere else.

Plainly something big and bad had stirred the anthill.

T'uga had become a port of refuge, and a highly profitable one now that Mercy and her ship, *The Grace*, had found both the becalmed *Resistance* and her thief, John Hicks, and towed them to this safe haven. The recollection had her rubbing her scarred right hand against her waistband. The old sword wounds had begun itching at the memory of their inception: when Hicks had not accepted her terms as easily as he might. Mercy had far too much invested in T'uga to endanger its existence.

'Something's wrong.' She said. 'I can smell it.'

\*

*'You wish our brother to atone for the wrongs he did you? That is your right. Llyr may not help you in this, though he will not stand in your way.'*

*'Should I not try? Evnissyen served us all a great wrong.'*

*'Would changing his fate make such a difference to the past wrongs? I doubt it.'*

*'I must do this, Bran ap Llyr.'*

*'What is done cannot be mended, Branwen. You of all here know that right is not always held by the mighty. But honour at least is on your side. You have my blessing to try. Yet to avenge your blood, Branwen, then you must spill his. If that is the course you have chosen I will provide you with a second chance. But he is not one to be bested easily.'*

*'I will fight him again,'* she replied. *'As often as needed, Bran ap Llyr. I do not fear what is to come. It is in the remembering that I find pain.'*

*'It pains you to recall?'*

*No, brother. When I feel pain it is already too late.'*

\*

'Ships astern.' The *Annika*'s steersman sang out, gesturing eastward.

Captain Awilda Synardus stared and swore. Pushing back the wisps of red hair escaping their tight braids, she shielded her eyes against the sun and read the clouds feathering westward in white-mackerel shafts. That at least was in her favour. 'If this bunch of slugs can shift us out beyond the headland we should make good time.'

The four ships under Awilda's command slid rapidly forward with each crew bending willingly to the oars. None questioned Awilda's choices of target or enemy. Woman or no, Awilda was her father's daughter. The sword that hung across her back and the vivid white scars across her right hand were testament to her fighting and survival skills. Awilda could hack and stab with the best of them.

'Captain.' Steinn glanced at her, an odd expression on his broad features. ''Tis himself.'

Awilda nodded. She needed no telling. Eivan's red and yellow wolf's head blazed across each closing sail like spilled blood and molten ore. She balanced lightly on the gunwale; one arm hooked around the carved prow, and stared toward the distant ships. 'Eivan Bransson, by Odin.' The man she would destroy for daring to approach her father with offers of marriage and drudgery to be forced upon her. That was no match for a daughter of kings. She bowed to no man, nor ran from him. Instead she had vowed to destroy him. Just as he had destroyed her home and family in return for her refusal.

Her ships were swift with the tide in their favour as they swung about to meet the enemy, and their silence was broken only by the *whap* of sail and sluice of oars across the dark, deep waters of the fiord. Then a chant was whispered somewhere in the flotilla. *Aa-wil-da*; each syllable drawn out in distinct separation. Sword hilts and javelins were thrummed against shields, softly at first, growing harder as the voices gained force. '*Aa-wil-da, Aa-wil-da, Aa-wil-da.*'

Across open water came a steady reply, '*Eiv-an, Eiv-an, Eiv-an*'.

Awilda stood in the prow, one hand aloft, and smiled at stray enemy arrows falling far short of them. Eivan did not have proper control of his crew and that could be to her advantage. She waited until arrows fell a bare arms-stretch from them. Only then did her fist drop, signalling the first stabbing volley into their enemy. She slipped from her vantage point to avoid the returning fire, leaving her proud Dragon-prows to snarl defiance at the opposing Wolves. Awilda barked the order to swing to port to avoid locking prows and becoming trapped. As starboard sides came broadside to each other, lines were thrown to snag the opposition's gunwales and draw them together into one huge battle arena.

Chants from each side roared out their defiance vying to overpower the other in sheer volume. Swords, javelins and shields clashed as the warriors from either side launched into hand to hand combat; chants now forgotten in the full-throated roar of a battle charge.

Awilda searched among the gore and armour for Eivan.

A sword thunked against her shield; she staggered back, parrying the blow with a sweeping stroke of her own. Her attacker landed another shattering blow and her shield cracked top to bottom. She threw it aside and hacked at him with a double-handed slash, severing both his sword arm and a goodly chunk of neck. Blood clouded her vision as arteries sprayed death across her face, but Awilda only wiped with the back of her hand and scooped up the fallen warrior's shield. Leapt across from one shallow hull to the next, blood rushing through her brain like a waterfall in the full-blown flood of spring thaw; singing in her head with the wailing howl of a Valkyrie calling her warriors to victory, or glorious Valhalla. She stabbed and slashed a path across two more hulls to the prow of the central ship and the man she had vowed to kill. She raised her sword high, staring Eivan in the eyes; pausing to savour the recognition she expected.

Too late she parried the double-handed slash which connected with her midriff and swept her over the gunwale into the churning, red-stained brine.

*

*'The sands will not run out just yet,' said Bran ap Llyr.*

*'Sands shift with the tides, and mainly on your whim,' Branwen replied. 'I did your bidding and claimed my reward. Yet you deny it me.'*

*'Not my bidding but yours, though I gave you my word. The time was wrong, sister. Chance comes to you again and he shall not walk away unchallenged.'*

*

Mercy pushed past Sheyn and concentrated on regaining her bearings. T'uga's inner workings morphed with the waxing and waning of dominant businesses that plied their dubious trade in the concourse. A different mix each time she returned, but always a thriving community. T'uga was a lucrative venture; even the few hundred guineas which Hicks bilked her for during her long absences was nothing against the security that this place gave her.

She could not recall exactly when the Dreadnaught's hulk had mutated into T'uga, nor whether it was the ship or the tiny planetoid on which it sat that was in truth T'uga. Confusion and lies were a habit with anything attached to John Hicks. Mercy hardly cared. The ship had been sufficiently disguised from the Admiralty still seeking their missing leviathan for many years now. T'uga it was now, with a mythology of its very own, populated by pirates and brigands and assorted low-lives from across the known and unknown universe. None cared what T'uga had been as long as it stayed free of Victoria's dominion; or that of Napoleon, or Lincoln, or any other of Homeworld's leaders.

That population, or at least those who bothered to notice her in their panic to leave, were regarding her now. Most with curiosity, a few with open hostility. She eased the sword that hung at her left hip, fingered the pearl-handled pistol that hung at her right; she also checked the knife on her belt and the small derringer in her sleeve before moving off. This being her home port she had not disembarked from *The Grace* fully armed. Checking the weapons that she did sport, however, was a subconscious act.

Nodding at Sheyn to follow, she moved across the concourse with that measured lilt of one more used to steel-framed grav-boots than the fancy thigh-high leather variety she sported today. Her eyes flickered toward the ceiling lenses just once and she resisted the temptation to flip them a finger; turning the move into a preening of the tangled red curls twisting from beneath her wide-brimmed hat. Real hair in a life-long spacer was a mere luxury; red hair was a rarity. For Mercy its rarity proved her lineage back to the Chieftain Eoghan Ó Máille and beyond. Mercedeys Benks was a living legend and she loved it.

The deck had begun to vibrate beneath her feet, as if flexing atrophied muscles. A distant hiss and chatter of engines rattled through the passages. That part of T'uga which was the *Resistance* had awoken. Mercy paused, frowning. Her scarred hand rubbed absent-mindedly at an itch under her belt. Yes, it was commercial sense to keep the power house of T'uga in running order, but this did not feel like a routine turning over of its vast engines. She placed a hand on the bulwark and felt the steady throb of a well-oiled engine shivering through her palm. She glanced back at the surveillance camera, openly this time, her head canted in query. Hicksey should know she was on guard.

Sheyn laid a warning finger to his lips. 'Gather what wits you have, lass. There's a storm a' brewing,' he whispered.

'Here?' She laughed. 'This is T'uga. And I'm not afeared of a little roughhousing.'

'Lass, there's a little blow and there's a solar wind. And if'n you trust that Cap'n's gut of yours you'll never be far enough adrift to roast alive.'

*

'*This should have ended Bran ap Llyr. It should have ended then.*'

'*The Wheel turns. Courage, Sister. Evnissyen will be*

*punished for his deeds and your son avenged.'*

*'It must end now.'*

*'Patience, Branwen. Your balance shall be gained. When the Wheel of Fate runs deep enough to find better purchase.'*

\*

Grainne toyed with her braided hair, its legendary red now streaked with grey. She looked around the deck, content despite a need for rubbing comfrey into the white scar on her right wrist that ached so damnably these past few years. Wind snapped extra canvas above her, and deck-boards creaked beneath her feet as the masts took up the strain, and her fast brigantine, *The Grace*, flew toward her prey.

Finding Eivan's small sloop was a surprise. She had followed his pirating trail for weeks now, and although she admired both his panache and appetite for spoils, she didn't like the cut of his jib on any other score.

'Load up the chain-shot,' she roared. 'Fire when ready, Master Gunner.'

'Aye, sir.'

Salvos of shot, chained in pairs, swirled toward the sloop's rigging. Whilst most fell wide, one coupled-missile swung its way into the mizzen, cracking the mast mid-length.

'Catch every breath, boys. She shan't gain port ahead of us. Earn your crust you slack-jawed vermin! Work your useless backsides or feel yer boson's lash!'

The gunners found their range; chain-shot smashed around the main mast and swept into the crowded mid-deck, cutting a swathe through the crew. The main-mast wavered, slowly arching downwards, its inexorable fall slowed by ropes and ladders and the damaged mizzen's wind-filled canvas. The sloop listed to port, trailing its broken mast in the ocean: a huge sculling oar, slicing water which was turning red with the blood of the fallen.

*The Grace* moved in for the kill, her slim hull skimming nimbly toward the crippled sloop, ploughing through smashed wood and human flotsam alike. The gunners had abandoned the cannons, not wanting to damage their prize more than necessary, and took to the deck guns, sending deadly blasts of metal fragments toward their wounded prey. Smoke wafted across the deck and stung Grainne's nose and she snuffled at it gleefully, allowing that distinctive and oh-so-familiar odour to taint her vision and sting her blood.

The sloop could not even limp for safety and was jerked around in a lazy spiral by the trailing masts. Shot peppered *The Grace*'s decks now as Eivan returned fire in the only manner left to him.

Gunpowder haze hung too thick for the light wind to disperse quickly. Gunshots merged into a contiguous chorus with the curdling, agonised cries of the wounded together.

'Prepare to repel boarders,' Eivan bellowed as the ships slid alongside. Boarding ropes and hooks snaked from *The Grace*'s rail.

Grainne checked her belt for her precious pistols and then hefted her sword and dirk in respective hands. *The Grace*'s crew were already swarming toward the sloop's deck and she was eager to join them.

"For, not to the age do I strive, nor for ever am I wroth, for the spirit from before me is feeble," she quoted grimly. 'And the souls I have made? For all the souls I have made are about to be joined by their brother!'

She dashed forward, clambering onto *The Grace*'s rail. She teetered there, looking toward the sloop; and down the barrel of a well-oiled pistol.

Eivan mouthed a last farewell as he pulled the trigger.

Grainne had no time to wonder. She was down between the hulls; sucking in blood-tainted brine with her final breath.

\*

*'The tides are turning, Branwen. He has found a current that can sweep him back.'*

*'As he has done so often before. He seems always to find a way, and I am tired, Bran ap Llyr.'*

*'The quest is yours to pursue, sister. Or not.'*

*'A blood oath I made, Brother. I must succeed. Given time.'*

*'Time is all you have, Branwen. Now at least he is out of his element.'*

*'If that be the case, then so am I, and we will both stand at risk.'*

\*

'Enough.' Mercy held a hand up for silence and listened intently for signs of life along the next corridor. It was oddly still beyond the engine rumble. Even the hubbub from the concourse had died away. She did not believe in coincidences; to her suspicious mind engines firing up the moment she stepped aboard smacked of arrogance and challenge.

The engine thrum slackened and she nodded satisfaction. 'With me,' she snapped, initially taking the companion way toward the cabin berth she retained on T'uga. Once clear of the concourse, however, she doubled back through the maze of corridors toward the bridge, with Sheyn close at her expensive boot heels.

They halted just one turn short of the bridge ladder. The engines were still idling, the soft *shush* and *kashomp* of the turning pistons slow and steady and, at this proximity, also very loud. The smell of soot was heavy in the air, and over that the dank, musty, unmistakable odour of ectoplasm. T'uga was preparing to fly.

At the sound of footsteps on the ladder, they hid in the nearest cabin. Mercy kept the door open a crack, pistol at the ready, watching as two sailors passed by. Both were trim and lithe, shaven-headed, clean-jawed and all-round well-washed. They could only be Navy; and her blood curdled.

'Trouble,' she grunted. 'Brace of Jack Tars.'

Sheyn crowded her shoulder for a glimpse. 'Just the brace?' he said.

'So far. Where the hell have they sprung from?'

Sheyn spread his hands. 'We've had no sightings of Admiralty ships for weeks.'

'We should've known that was odd just on its own.' Mercy opened the door a little further and checked the corridor. The crewmen had rounded the corner. They would be setting up sentry duty on the bridge ladder. 'So Hicksey is expecting us,' she said. 'I am going to skewer that little rodent.'

'Unless I get to him first,' Sheyn replied.

'We need another way up to the bridge.' She grinned at her companion. 'Through the Captain's Sea Cabin. Hicksey's own state rooms. Follow me.' She slipped away from the bridge ladders toward the officers' quarters.

The further they crept along strangely deserted

corridors the more Mercy's instincts were rattled. If the Admiralty truly had taken the bridge then T'uga was no longer a safe haven. The question she asked herself was: had they come in with or without Hicksey's help. He would do almost anything to rid himself of Mercy and her hold both on him and T'uga. But handing over his biggest asset and risking arrest? Whatever the whys and wherefores of her ex-partner's involvement, it was certain she would not be allowed off the ship voluntarily. Which brought her to the next question: how many were there? Doubtless a naval vessel was hidden somewhere nearby, but they had to have arrived in a small ship. Which meant a small task force. Her most obvious option was to cripple the command and then make a run for open space.

Near the end of the final ladder leading into Hicks's rooms stood a sentry in naval slops and bellbottoms. So Hicks's own domain was under guard. Did that mean the Navy weren't here by invitation?

The engines' hum changed once more: turning faster, approaching running speed. Whatever her business partner's situation, the Navy seemed set to reinstate T'uga as Victoria's Dreadnaught.

'With or without you, Hicksey my old shipmate.' Mercy drew her small knife and inched forward, signalling Sheyn to cover the far side of the corridor. She needed the ensign to look away, however briefly; a raised voice from the deck above gave her the chance she looked for. He looked up, his well-shaven throat exposed, and Mercy lived up to repute by showing none of her name's sake. Sheyn helped her drag the twitching corpse into the nearest doorway, propping it there. The blood trail could not be hidden, but she hoped this would not matter very soon.

Tweaking out the dead sailor's pistol and knife, Mercy tucked them into her belt and ran to the ladder. Climbing silently, she reached the top and peered across the bridge to assess her opponents. There were three naval ratings on deck, and two officers. And Hicksey standing close to the helm. That answered her first question.

Mercy slipped up the last few steps and dodged into the deserted Coms recess, followed swiftly by Sheyn.

One rating rested his hands on the wheel while the others stood ready at the engine controls. The officers were gathered together, their attention fixed on the small bank of screens to the helm's left, and away from Mercy.

'I see nothing of her, Hicks.' The Commander was young. His pips and braid achingly new on jacket and hat. So young that she wondered how he was ever worthy of rank at all.

'Eivan Bransson,' she muttered. 'Viscount Bransson's youngest brat. Damn his blood.'

'The Honourable Eivan,' Sheyn added. 'A sneakier rat never walked any deck! Honourable—'

Mercy motioned him to silence, intent now on the room's occupants.

'...then worry,' Hicks was saying. 'When it comes to survival, Mercy Benks has the instincts of a cockroach. Once we're all stardust, there she'll be, plying the stars.'

'One woman against Her Majesty's Navy.' Eivan's tone left Mercy in no doubt what he thought of that idea. 'No matter. *The Resistance* is our goal, Mr Hicks. Mercedeys Benks can wait.'

Hicks made no further comment but grinned and

shook his head slowly.

Eivan signalled the ensign. 'Are we ready to cast off, Mr Lane?'

'Yes, sir. Warlocks are powering up the engines and awaiting your orders. *The Reliant* has left cover and is moving into position as escort.'

'Excellent. Then lift off; and slow ahead, if you please.'

The young officer turned, his face pale. 'But sir, the exiles are still leaving. You gave your word on their safety...'

Eivan stared back – a cold glance. 'I said we would leave when it was safe for us to do so. We needn't concern ourselves with a little scum floating above decks. Most would be bound for the gallows in any event.' He stepped back to get a full view of the screens forward. 'Mr Lane?' he prompted.

'Casting off, sir. Engines slow ahead.'

As he spoke the engine note changed, deepening, guttural and laboured. The decks juddered, rocking wildly for a moment; lurching to port.

From outside Mercy could hear faint noises of tearing and grinding and shouted warnings. She could imagine the pandemonium in the concourse as those attempting to flee T'uga hurled themselves clear; many to certain death as *The Resistance* rose quickly, ripping free of its camouflage of silt, debris and squalor, built up over its many years aground.

The view on screen changed from crags and rifts to clear, dark, sky.

'Full ahead,' Eivan snapped.

'Full ahead, sir.'

Engines vibrated as the reborn *HMS Resistance* leaped

upward and forward. The screen darkened to the eternal night of space.

Mercy signed to Sheyn: which of the Navy men should be the first to die: which of them she wanted. They needed no words after so many battles, so many brawls, so many ships.

Now it was time. She could feel it.

*The Resistance* was heading into ectopic-slippage. In a few minutes it would slither through the universe in a pale wave of ectoplasmic shimmer. If she did not act, *The Grace* would be left far behind, and regardless how much affection Mercy had for T'uga she loved *The Grace* – and loved her freedom even more.

With a howl she bounded forward, despatching the steersman in one move. Whirling around, she brought her cutlass slashing across the Number One's throat before both of her booted feet had returned to deck.

She saw Sheyn plunge a knife in another crewman's kidneys before leaping toward the second. She had time to think how efficient he was for his age, when a shot rang out at close range. Lead ripped through her; she felt it tearing her gut out through her back. The controls would be covered…

A second shot struck her.

Eivan was gaping, wild-eyed and terrified; still pointing a pistol at her belly. She eyed the space between them, wondering if she was still capable of making a lunge at him before he got off another shot. She could see Sheyn across the room, holding Hicks at bay, just waiting for her to give the word to finish him.

'Hold!' Eivan shouted. 'Or your captain dies.'

Mercy raised her hands slowly to shoulder height,

palms out in the traditional gesture of surrender. 'You fire again young pup, and we may all die.' She smiled grimly, wincing at the pain her raised arms gave to her shattered gut.

'I take no orders from a pirate.'

He was shaking; she could see the tip of the barrel waver, almost smell his fear. She lowered her hands as slowly as she had raised them. 'Don't be a fool, Eivan.'

'From your lips, Benks, it's Lord Bransson,' he replied.

'Oh, Eivan, such formality. After our last meeting I hoped we could be friends.'

'I am no friend to a thief and a pirate.'

'Then I am sorry for you, lad.' She let her hand slide toward her belt and the dagger concealed there. 'You might want to put the gun down.'

'You are not in a position to dictate.'

'Perhaps not, but I can try to even the odds a little.' Mercy flipped the dagger from her belt, sending it stabbing through the space between them, piercing Eivan's chest and heart.

Maybe it was muscle contraction, perhaps instinct. Eivan's finger jerked the pistol's trigger, returning a sphere of lead toward his killer.

She felt the control panel behind her warming with the sudden leaking of ectoplasm, and she had time enough to wonder how so much valuable fuel came to be amassed so far from Earth before the bridge erupted into quivering and insubstantial shadow. The ship wavered between the solidity of present existence and its far-distant destination, before becoming a mass of swirling debris ringed by dissipating ectoplasmic shock waves, eddying out toward the void.

Cold; the intense chill of nothingness all around her. Adrift amid the flotsam that had been *The Resistance*, she turned slowly and watched the hulk drift away from her, spewing chunks of metal and wood into the universe, like breadcrumbs strewn across a pond. Her hat had drifted away, and her red hair floated free in a blood-red halo that wrapped around her pale face; her last – her final – vision.

# Princess Born

A FIRE CRACKLED in the Library's out-sized grate thickening the air so that everything but sleep seemed such an effort. Prince Adras lounged back in his chair, long legs thrust out across the rug before him, flicked another playing card at his older brother's discarded coronet. The Knave of Hearts slid over the rim to settled face-up in the centre and he smiled.

The next card skittered across the table and onto the *Book of Native Fauna* that was the object of his brother, Crown Prince Clovis's attention. 'How about a jaunt out to the lakes?' he murmured. 'Bag a few ducks maybe? Or a spot of fishing?' He flicked an imaginary cast into the centre of the room, scattering the remainder of the deck in a wide arc before him.

Clovis lifted his head in bemused affront at the interruption. 'Ducks?'

'Ducks.' Adras agreed. 'You know, quack, quack?' He flapped his hands limply at his sides.

Clovis considered the word carefully. 'Ducks,' he repeated. 'Stopped raining has it?'

'Hours ago.'

'Right then.' The book snapped shut. 'Hobbs?'

'Sir.'

'We're going to the lakes. Get my stuff.'

'But your Mother. The Queen was quite clear about

staying in the grounds... Of course, Sir. At once.' Hobbs paused at the door. 'Will you require a Captain's escort?'

'To the lake? It's not even out of sight of the walls. Anyway, you can't take those clods out for a hunt. Bloody great boots stamping about frightening fish and fowl for miles. Just a footman or three, thank you Hobbs.'

Hobbs stiffened, but swallowed the reprimand he would have given when the Princes were younger. 'As the young Sir wishes.'

Clovis allowed one of his rare grins. 'Ducks it is brother,' he said. 'But my turn first.'

*

'Really Clovis. Do get a move on. Dammed birds will start roosting before I fire a shot.' Adras leaned on his gun rest, and shifted awkwardly where he lay in the tangle of tall reeds. They had an excellent view of the water, and of the Eiders and Mallards idling among the reeds and lilies.

Clovis nodded without looking round. Discarded sheets lay in a heap by his left elbow, a box of charcoal and pastels by his right, as he scribbled lines and colour onto yet another version of the scene before them.

Adras couldn't mind the wait after he had suggested Clovis came along, but he wanted to get a shot or two in before dark. To his mind Clovis had so many sketches by now he didn't actually 'need' the birds to paint them.

The footman crouched close by cleared his throat and pointed across the marsh at two figures struggling toward them. Female and rather shapely ones at that. Adras raised himself up for a better look.

'Hellooooo!' The short, well-rounded red-head waved

not just her raised arm, but her entire body, with her bellowed greeting.

The water erupted in a flurry of sound as birds fled, fearing for their lives, and Adras could only stare after them. He raised the gun half-heartedly, but they had already vanished. 'Damn. If I'd been looking at them when that darned woman screeched I might have potted a few.'

'Hellooooo!' the red-head howled again. Closer now he could see her cheery face and voluptuous chest bobbing toward them through the long grass. Birds forgotten, his only audible reaction was a ghostly exclamation of, 'Gosh'.

Clovis was less inhibited. His normal reticence scattered along with the ducks. 'Who are you, and what the hell do you want? Clear orf, dammit.'

The red-head ploughed forward, undeterred. Adras noted how, despite the flounces and lace of her dress, her sensible boots allowed relatively unhindered progress through grass and mud. Her blonde companion tottered at an ever-increasing distance behind her; finally halting when her skimpy 'heels' were sucked from her feet by the glutinous earth.

'We're lost,' the red-head hollered, though she was close enough not to. 'Party trip, don't you know. Seeing Her Majesty's Secretary and all that.'

Clovis groaned quietly and turned his back on them. Adras could hardly blame him. Both knew what that meant. A fresh hoard of potential brides to be vetted by the family firm.

Adras had fewer problems than his brother, the heir apparent. He bowed graciously and motioned the footman forward to assist the ladies onto firmer ground. The red-head plunged forward unaided, but the other hesitated, simpering as the flunky delicately lifted her free of the mud and ferried her onto the bank. Adras grimaced as the servant returned to grope in the slurry for the shoes that had fallen free of her shapely feet, and nodded approval when the offending footwear was found.

'Good man,' he called loudly. 'Jolly good show.' He beamed as if he personally had been their rescuer and then knelt to assist with the shoe's fitting.

'Thanks most awfully Your Highness,' the blonde whispered to him. 'So terribly kind.'

'No trouble.' His attention was taken by the red head, who had retrieved his gun, and was shouldering it with great confidence as a lone Eider fluttered onto the pond's rippled surface. She pulled both barrels in rapid succession, bagging not only the first bird, but a second that he had not even seen just flitting into range on the farther side. Both birds splashed into the water.

Adras instinctively waved at the dogs to 'fetch'. 'Jolly good,' he breathed, awestruck. 'Good shooting old girl.'

'Thanks.' She laughed loudly. A deep braying that made Clovis shake his head in disbelief.

Adras, however, was entranced. 'Jolly good.' He repeated. 'Absolutely wonderful.'

'Steady on,' Clovis muttered. He turned to the blonde and offered her one of his paint cloths to wipe her mud covered feet.

'So kind,' she simpered. 'Sorry to be a frightful nuisance, but you couldn't show us back to the castle could you? A path that isn't so terribly mucky?'

'Oh … yes … of course.' He waved his footman forward. 'George, help the young lady to the path will you?'

'Highness.' The footman moved in, waiting her nod of acceptance before lifting her through the reeds to firmer ground.

Clovis followed with his easel and papers. 'All right?' he asked her.

She nodded.

'Jolly good. George, bring the rest will you? There's a good chap.' He inclined his head to the blonde. 'Clovis,' he said. 'And you are?'

'Dorcas.' She curtsied low, her head bowed. 'I am so sorry Your Highness, we had no idea…'

'No,' he smiled, twitching his fingers to indicate she should rise. 'Well, let's get back and get you cleaned up. Can't have you meeting Mother in that state, can we?' He looked back suddenly. 'Will your friend be okay? Does she need help?'

'No Your Highness.' She giggled suddenly, hiding her mouth behind her slender fingers. 'Samira's used to all the outdoor stuff. Her daddy's a cavalry officer.'

'Oh?' He looked back at Samira.

Snatches of her chatter came drifting to him over the reed beds. 'What fun … can't always get decent dogs though … bagged ten brace that afternoon…'

He shrugged at Dorcas and grinned. 'You two are friends?' he murmured.

'Oh yes. We *finished* together. Very good academy. Terribly select.'

He nodded gravely. From old families, then, who taught their daughters to be ladies above all else. 'I say,' he said. 'If you don't do the huntin'n'shootin' thing, do you play croquet?'

'Rather.' She smiled and after a suitably coy and meaningful hesitation, as befitted a lady, took his proffered hand so that he might help her along the rough path toward the royal abode. 'Yes, indeed. I've always preferred ball games.'

\*

'She's not royal my dear, that is why.' The Queen snapped the book shut and glared at her eldest son, daring him to argue.

'By whose measure?' he demanded. 'Just because some damned book says so?' He stared out of the window, hands clasped behind his back. The gardens were in full evening shadow, and he could only just make out the white hoops of metal and cane on the croquet lawns. But looking out at a darkening garden was better than trying to face down Mother when she was determined to be right.

'Debrights are always correct in these things,' she said. 'Don't contradict me, boy.'

'Dorcas is in Succession.' Clovis muttered.

'Just. By a hound's whisker,' she waved a handful of small portraits under his nose.

'So if they're so bloody unsuitable why invite them in the first place?'

'Oh don't be so bloody naive, boy. Red top scrolls are demanding we give the lower levels a sniff of the prize at the very least. But these?' She waved at the portraits once more. 'These are Princesses born and bred, and not a scandal within twenty miles of them.'

'I could say the same about my horse,' he snapped. 'In

fact,' he swivelled the pictures around to scrutinise them carefully. 'I think they might be related, they've got the same teeth.'

'Don't be rude about your cousins, dear.' The Queen held each picture up to the lamplight and examined them minutely. 'We shall see who's right in the morning.'

'Oh God, not that stupid test,' he groaned.

'It's traditional. Tradition is what keeps us what we are,' she replied carefully. 'If you change it for the sake of your own whim it ceases to be heritage. It will come back on you in the end.'

'Rubbish Mother. It's superstitious garbage. And hardly a tradition if it hasn't been done for the past six generations. Why start again now?'

'It has not been required for the past six generations. Your forebears have all had more dammed sense. But no matter. We shall see if this is all nonsense in the morning. Now I am tired.' She tilted her head to proffer her cheek toward her sons.

'Good night mother,' Clovis leant over to kiss her dutifully. 'Goodnight Clovis. Sleep well. Goodnight Adras.' Her second son also kissed her lightly on the cheek before both withdrew from her presence.

'What now?' Adras groaned. 'They won't get through tomorrow.'

Clovis drifted back to the window, silent for a few moments as he stared across the crochet lawns once more and a slow smile spread across his face. 'Won't they?' He turned to slap his brother's shoulder. 'I think they might.' He clapped his brother on the back again, harder this time. 'Breeding will out, and all that.'

*

The Queen sat at the end of the vast throne room. The Chancellor stood just behind her holding a lengthy scroll of names. To her right sat Prince Clovis and on left was Adras. None were in good humour. The Queen, because neither son had shown any interest in her choices, and the sons for exactly the opposite reason.

The Chancellor had the unenviable task of choosing the candidates with the view to pleasing both sides and decided that no one could meet the needs of this family. He had interviewed the Queen's choices, and had them dismissed by her sons, though at least half had met with requirements

The royal personages did not argue. That was bad form in front of the subjects. They just chose not to agree. And as their irritation grew, so their conversations grew shorter. So short that waiting girls were barely setting foot on the Throne Room's marble floor before being dismissed.

'Princess Evelyn and Princess Armina,' the Queen had said.

'No,' Clovis grunted.

'Or me,' Adras added.

The Chancellor sent a footman to intercept the two Princesses before they too were humiliated by their slow progress toward the throne and even slower reversing to the anteroom where ten or more previously rejected blue -bloods were shedding tears and curses in equal quantity.

The Chancellor cleared his throat impatiently and looked to Her Majesty to admit the remaining two candidates. She sighed heavily and shrugged, flicking the fingers of her right hand without lifting her wrist from the throne's great wooden arms rests; a tired, wordless, *yes*.

'The Duchess Dorcas of Kinley and the Honourable Miss Samira Wentworth-Piers,' the Chancellor bellowed. The doors parted and the two girls entered. They paused to curtsy to the floor before advancing at the required slow-step across the pattered marble.

'Not royal,' the Queen said abruptly. 'Unacceptable.'

'She's a Duchess,' said Clovis. 'I told you that.'

'A long way down the list,' she replied tartly. 'So far down it would take several plagues, and an earthquake to get her name onto the bottom of the third scroll.'

'Not the point,' Clovis replied. 'If she passes the test you can't say another thing. It was your idea after all.'

'I say,' Adras hissed. 'Keep it down. They're getting a bit close.'

'Agreed, Mother?' Clovis laid a hand on the armrest and looked her in the eyes. 'Is it?'

'Agreed,' she sighed.

The girls had come to a halt before the dais and with heads bowed they dropped into deepest of curtseys.

'Rise,' the Queen called. 'I will ask you questions, and you will answer truthfully. No matter what. Do you understand?'

Obediently the girls rose and looked straight at her. They nodded, like a pair of slack stringed marionettes.

'Right, so first question, did you sleep well?' the Queen enquired.

'Your Highness?' Dorcas said.

'I asked if you slept well,' the Queen said, more sharply. *Instinct*, she thought. *These two will never do.*

'Well? Did you?' she asked a third time.

'Well actually Your Highness ... it wasn't that comfy. I mean, the bed was so high up I needed a step-ladder. And ... it was terribly lumpy.'

'Lumpy?' the Queen demanded.

'Er, well.' Dorcas flushed red. 'Well. Your Highness. That is, well I expect it's just being in a strange bed. I mean to say...'

'Never mind child.' The Queen snarled. 'And you ... Saminta.'

'Samira your Highness.' Samira bowed her head and curtsied briefly. 'I slept well enough Your Highness.'

Clovis took in a breath sharply and shook his head very slightly. Samira looked from mother to son, her lower jaw working up and down soundlessly as she fought to find an answer that would appease both of them.

Her friend saved her the bother. 'What utter rot Sammi,' Dorcas chimed in. 'You were up and down all night. I heard you.' She blushed.

'It was fine,' Samira said. 'Once I'd swapped beds with my maid.'

'And?' the Queen snapped. 'Obviously there is more. Tell the truth, child. I will not be lied to.'

Dorcas drew a breath, her focus flickering toward Samira for a briefest moment. Then she leaned toward the throne to add, 'I've some terrible bruises, begging your pardon Your Majesty,' She dropped a deep curtsy. 'Well you did say the truth, no matter what.'

'I did.' The Queen gestured toward the exit and looked over the girl's heads; her face was strained and taught so that her lips barely moved. 'You may leave.'

Samira and Dorcas hesitated for a merest second before rising to back away from the throne.

The royal trio said nothing until they had gone.

'Well Clovis,' the Queen said finally. 'You appear to have won your argument. If you will excuse me?' She rose and swept from the room in a flurry of high dudgeon and watered silk.

'Gosh,' Adras breathed. 'Mother's not happy.'

'Would you be?' Clovis leapt to his feet and beckoned Adras to follow. 'I say we should check those mattresses before the maids unmake the beds.'

'Huh?'

'Beds, Adras,' Clovis said patiently. 'The beds. A little matter of peas?'

'Oh. Yes. Odd that. I thought they'd fall down on that one. Proper Princesses and all that.'

'So did I,' Clovis agreed. 'So we need to deal with the PEAS. You know? The special peas?'

'Oh?' Adras said, confused by his brother's suddenly furtive manner. 'You think they didn't have any peas after all?'

'Yes Adras. Of course they had peas.' Clovis looked sidelong at his brother and winked. 'What did you think I'd use? Croquet balls?'

# Wind Blows the Oaks

Tearing flesh,
though osmosis.
Soaring and flowing,
a dull blade that
in a single sound
brings exquisite pain.

What once was,
is gone.
As an ebbing tide
it plunges,
bending ancients,
until, the rain comes,

Jousting, careless,
Dryad, telling all
the remains.
Spellbound.
new leaves dance.
and are … lost.

# Pet Therapy

'BASTARD. BASTARD. FETCH the cart. Bastard. Bastard. Shut up Robbie. Shut up. Bastard.'

Molly frowned at the dark beyond the window and then swivelled her electric chair around for a peek at Reception. There was no one in sight and the only sounds came from Robbie the macaw, squawking hysterically from the Residents' Lounge

Pet therapy had been a staple of the eight-bed Honeywood Hospice for a long while. Volunteers brought their dogs and moggies in for an afternoon of hugs and strokes, giving many people comfort. Where a moth-eaten, foul-beaked macaw came into the mix was, for many residents and visitors, far less obvious. Personally, Molly had found the bird refreshingly anarchic; to be relied upon for those apt asides that made her smile in a way that very little did these days.

'Probably that cat winding him up. He and Chomi aren't exactly tight.' Will let out a small grunt and sigh as he moved to a more comfortable spot in a hospital bed too short for his close-on two metre frame. 'I wish he'd let an old man sleep.'

'Bet nobody's covered his cage.' Molly said. 'But I like hearing him, Will. He's for people like us.'

'Speak for yourself.' Will settled into the battery of pillows and closed his eyes. His hand, clamped around the morphine trigger, twitched once, twice, a third time for luck. Within seconds he was oblivious.

Molly glanced around Will's room with its family pictures and books. A study more befitting an educated man of advanced age than a death-bed setting. Molly was surprised at the friendship that had grown between them given their age difference, and as surprised at how attached she had become to this building and the people in it. Not the depressing place she had imagined when she first been sent here for respite care. Her parent's respite, she realised, and not her own. She was only angry that the creeping canker in her blood led to this incarceration. Honeywood was full of that contradiction and yet also awash with optimism and courage and very little fear. Death could never be evaded; it was here in all its raw essence, but what Honeywood lacked was the antiseptic, clinical, treating-the-meat, kind of thing; patients were not subjected to a constant battery of tests and consultants. Both were caring in their way but a production line of medical procedure, nevertheless. Here it was all about the time and the space to just *be*. She could not imagine why she had not come here sooner, other than her own fears, of course.

She looked out at the night once again and then back through to the corridor. Robbie was still shrieking. She had been here long enough to know an absence of staff meant just one thing; someone had gone. 'Has to be Hilda,' she said. 'Poor old dear's been teetering all day.' Will didn't move, or even appear notice her. He was away for the night.

She manoeuvred her wheelchair round and listened to hushed voices drifting along the corridor. It was a pale-sage tunnel that stretched through the building from main entrance to the carefully-shaded conservatory designated as the residents' communal room. It was dotted with local art and strategically placed flora, and without the inevitable spatter of notices and warning signs and pair of fire doors, currently and illicitly propped open, it could be a high class hotel, or a spa, or even a larger than average house; provided that house came with reception desk as standard, plus industrial-sized potted plants.

Molly trundled toward the conservatory and stopped just outside. She reached behind her seat for the forearm crutches tucked into their clips and heaved herself upright with reasonable ease and minimal pain.

'Robbie, what's the racket?' She needn't have asked. The cause of Robbie's outburst sat on the dining table staring right back at the bird.

Chomi, as Will had named her, was long and lean, with the unmistakable wedge-shaped head and over-sized ears of an Abyssinian queen-cat. Its huge copper-coloured eyes, set in short fur of the deepest, glossiest black, were now fixed on Molly. Calculating, feline eyes. Chomi yowled that grating, deep yow, like no other breed could ever make. She yawned, her dark tongue curling like a small scarlet rug, and then poured herself down to the floor. One final scitching moan at the bird and she wafted away at a measured stroll. Her skinny, black tail was held high with its tip kinked slightly, as though it had been broken and badly mended.

Molly always got the impression it was Chomi's version of 'flipping a finger'. She watched the cat drift off on some engrossing feline mission and wondered how it had got into the building after security had cleared for the night. *But then*, she thought, *cat. Ergo, a question that was neither relevant nor possessed of an answer*. Chomi, Will had told her, meant friend in his native Cape Town. Molly really had some doubts on that score.

Robbie ceased his torrent of abuse the moment Chomi left and was busily re-arranging his mangy feathers, pausing only to tilt his all-seeing gaze in Molly's direction as she swayed across the room. 'Fuck off,' he muttered. 'Fetch the crash cart.'

'Bastard,' Molly whispered through the bars and reached for the thick, tattered, cage drape. Robbie got in a final 'fuck-off' as the cover dipped him into darkness, and was silent beyond the faint scritch-scratch of that nut -cracking beak.

'Molly?' The light was snapped on by Beth Cho, the night shift's senior duty nurse, a rangily built, Indonesian Staff Nurse in her fifth decade. 'What are you doing still up,' she said. 'You haven't taken your medication have you? Oh Molly, you're here to rest, my dear.'

'Drugs don't help much,' Molly replied. 'And Will wanted to talk.'

'I know, but you should still rest.'

Molly nodded, and then jerked her head toward the resident's rooms 'Hilda?'

'Yes,' said Beth. 'She was a DNR. Nothing we could do, and she's been in a lot of pain.'

Molly nodded, flopping heavily into the electric wheelchair. She was more tired in body than she cared to let show, but her mind was water on a hot-plate, skittering across every corner at once. 'Beth was busy teasing that cat just an hour ago,' she said.

'I know. We had to put it out when her monitors went off.'

'So she came down to annoy Robbie.'

'I know that as well. Heaven knows how that animal got in after hours. I must have words with the manager. There is pet therapy and there's a bloody nuisance. But Hilda seemed to want the company, so...' She raised her shoulders, hands spread at an unanswerable question.

'Chomi was here on Sunday night when Carol went,' Molly said. 'Is it me or does that animal somehow seem to *know* when people are ... you know...'

'They do say animals sense these things. Don't go saying that too loudly though, or we'll have patients keeling over every time they see that creature walk past their room.'

Molly was never sure what was gallows humour, and what wasn't, with Beth. The woman seemed genuinely upset, so she nodded and said nothing. Beth Cho was a constant in this small world of changing faces and there was no call to upset her. 'I don't know where Chomi went,' she said. 'Better keep an eye on Robbie though. That cat probably thinks he's her next snack.'

Molly went to bed, submitting meekly to the tags and monitors she worked so hard to avoid in waking hours. Hilda's death had shocked her. *True, she was – had been – an old woman*, Molly thought, *but she was here for respite, like me*. Molly hated the idea that maybe the old woman had decided it was time. It went against every instinct she'd had. But life was never so simple. *Sometimes people got tired, very tired*, she thought, and slipped quickly into sleep.

*Something pressed down on her, squeezing the air from fragile lungs – and there was a sweetness to it. Pain was receding and calm ran through her that she hadn't known for a long while.*

Molly told herself to open her eyes. *This had to be it, she thought, the out of body thing that Will had been going on about.*

The idea of seeing her own body from somewhere up amongst the light fittings wasn't what she wanted. She wanted to live, and a part of her consciousness screamed at herself not to accept this. But an unfamiliar euphoria had crept across her spirit that made it seem worth while.

*A tingling that was sensuous, exciting. Something breathing close to her face. She could feel moisture on her lips; not breath, but a kiss. She could feel at last and she felt good. A gentle urgency raising her nerve endings out of their drug-cushioned fog. Rumbling, like a small engine, so close the vibrations shivered through her neck and shoulders.*

Molly's eyes flickered open. She gained a glimpse of half closed eyes staring back in that deep well of sound; coppery eyes in a sharp, midnight face.

*The mist closed over her once more. High-pitched whining had joined the chorus that meant something. Something important she could not identify. Friction, still, against her lips, faster now, and close to harsh. Raised voices infiltrated her re-discovered euphoria and she wanted them to go away. They were telling her to fight back; pulling her from the warm comfort she was offered. Molly parted her lips and strained forward...* And found nothing.

The pressure on chest and lips had ceased abruptly and Beth Cho was there, rubbing her hands and arms, and calling her name.

Molly clawed briefly at the air line under her nose as consciousness flooded her lobes. A few breaths, as deep as her rattling lungs would allow, and she was back.

'Molly. Can you understand me? Molly. Wake up. Come on. Molly.' Beth was massaging Molly's hands almost to the point of pain in an effort at waking her patient.

The girl clasped Molly's digits into stillness, and whispered, 'What happened?'

'Your monitors kicked off. You're stabilised now. Are you in pain?'

'No pain. Well, no more than usual. It was a dream. I was dreaming so clearly.'

'Ah. The nightmares.'

'No. It was a good dream. Peaceful. I didn't want to wake up, but there was a noise. And something on my face.'

Beth looked back through the open doorway.

It was the minutest of gestures but Molly had grown adept at reading things people *didn't* say around her. Those things people always assumed she wasn't ready to know. Moving her head a little she peered around the nurse. The only thing to see was Chomi sitting in the centre of the corridor, washing her oversized ears with that casual feline nonchalance. *So at home, even though she didn't actually live here.*

'Well you did say people keeled over. But not me. Not yet.' Molly managed a small laugh. 'Cat, nil – me, one.'

'Don't tempt fate. I called security to have it removed earlier, but they couldn't find it.'

'Well she's here now. Have you tried calling the

RSPCA?'

'They wouldn't come out. They didn't have an officer to spare.' Beth crinkled her mouth, looking all around her in short jabbing tilts of her head, obviously nervous. 'They wouldn't find a demon. It's a devil cat, that one. Chordewa.' She cut off sharply, a faint, fleeting flush tinting her cheeks. 'Don't listen to me. Spouting superstitions from my grandmother's knee. Forget it.' She smoothed Molly's arm. 'No point offering you something to help you sleep? Didn't think so. I shall check back on you in a little while.' She straightened the covers and hurried away leaving Molly with more questions than ever.

Chomi was still out there, right in middle of the corridor, washing those satellite-dish ears. Nobody knew where Chomi came from, though being so sleek and glossy she was quite obviously no street urchin. But a demon? Chomi paused her ablutions to return Molly's stare with cool, copper-coloured eyes, and then slipped somehow from view without appearing to move.

Molly smiled at the naivety in Beth's hints. A demon? Ridiculous. More than a little mad. Yet... She waited to be sure Beth was not lingering close by before reaching for her iPad. She searched for cats that might fit the bill, starting with 'Black Abyssinians' that, she learned, did not come in black. They were a darkish grey. The truly black Bombay Cat was a modern cross-breed. Interesting, but not helpful. She Googled cat gods and demons and got the usual suspects: Mafdet, Mau, Bast, Kasha, Shasti. There was quite a list but none fitted, at least not according to the websites she found.

Molly put the pad on sleep and lay back, wondering

what else she could ask. The bed juddered and Chomi was standing on the quilt, gazing intently at her, and vibrated a rusty greeting. In that instant Molly was afraid. Hard not to be when Beth, and now she, had the animal down as a creature of ill omen.

Chomi regarded her in silence and then crouched to knead at Molly's dressing gown, which lay across the end of the bed. The cat's eyes narrowed and she began to purr. It was the sound of any normal cat and Molly had to smile. There are few sounds harder to resist than a cat's purr. She reached forward to touch the creature's head. Their gazes connected again. The purr changed gear, becoming a low grumble, close to, but not quite, the fractured growl of a Siamese, but deeper and less feline, like no other cry Molly had ever heard. It wavered on, a continuous, sinuous, **susurration,** insistent as the wailing of a siren, yet calming, mesmerising, as sirens were not. It grated on Molly's senses, yet somehow soothed her toward sleep.

A trolley loaded with breakfast crockery, heralding approaching dawn and the day shift, rattled out along the corridor. Its clatter broke the moment. *Shattering the spell*, Molly thought. She snatched her hand back in the moment that Chomi turned her alien head toward the noise.

Molly kicked out hard beneath the quilt, launching the cat into clear air. It landed near the door, crouched low, head outstretched, eyes a shade of deeper flame. For a moment Molly thought it would leap back to her, and then the trolley jangled once more, closer this time, paces from the open door. With a parting glottal spit the cat disappeared, so fast Molly had no idea which direction it had taken, but was monumentally relieved it had gone. Beth's demon-cats were suddenly far less bizarre.

Molly went back to Googling on her iPad.

*

After a slow search of the whole floor, peering in to each patient, family and staff room in turn, Molly retreated to the Residents' Lounge. 'You did see it?' she asked Will. 'Last night. Did you see anything?'

'Chomi? Yes.'

'Where? When?'

'In the corridor. When you were shouting.'

'I was shouting?'

He grinned. 'My room is opposite. Believe me, you were screaming.'

'But you saw the cat.'

Will nodded. 'For a few seconds, and then it just vanished. Poof!' He pinched and splayed his fingers to demonstrate. 'Took off so fast.'

'Which way?'

Will stared at her for a moment, 'Which way did what?'

'How did it vanish? *Star Trek* or Cheshire Cat style?'

He picked at his lower lip for a moment and shook his head. 'Neither. It vanished, as in, it wasn't there any more.'

'So supernatural fast,' she said. 'I thought I'd imagined it.'

Clattering in the doorway made them pause: a cleaner with her trolley. An Asian woman of indeterminate age; pretty with her high-cheeked, features and a permanent half smile that Molly would have placed more readily on some temple Goddess than a domestic.

'Good afternoon, Mrs C,' Will said. 'Lovely day.'

The woman smiled, before darting off to clear the single discarded newspaper littering a table.

'She's late,' Molly murmured, embarrassed at her jitters.

'She often is. She's got three jobs you know.'

Molly watched the woman trot around the room, dusting and tidying and rubbing vigorously at spotless table tops. Her nan had been a cleaner and she could appreciate the work that people never saw and took for granted. *But still,* Molly thought. *I'm sure she's already been in here today.*

'This cat,' she said to Will, 'did you actually see it sitting on my bed? Before I shouted out. I think...' She looked away for a moment. 'I don't expect you to believe me, but I think this is a Chordewa. A devil cat.'

'A what?'

Molly handed over her iPad, pointing at the page blooming into view.

'Chordewa,' he read. 'Demon whose soul leaves her body in the guise of a black cat. Yeah, right. Course it is.'

'I knew you wouldn't believe me. But when it was sitting on my chest. And taking me away.'

'A cat stealing your breath.'

'Not quite, but close.' Molly poured tea into the mugs. The simple act was another convenient distraction. What she was saying was nonsense on the surface. Her other nan, not the cleaning one, always claimed cats stole your breath in your sleep. 'You don't believe me?' she asked.

'I do, as it happens.' Will picked at the loose threads on his blanket as the silence ticked between them. 'It's not a real animal. We need to destroy it before takes another soul.'

'Now you're sounding like a vicar.'

Will tapped his chest 'Card-carrying altar boy. Does that count?'

Molly grinned and looked back at the iPad. 'I can't find much on it, though. Every site seems to quote the same sources. *Chordewa is a demon who seeks out the sick and dying.*'

'A cat could hardly eat a whole person.'

'Doesn't eat the flesh. Listen to this. *Chordewa kills by licking the victim's lips and inhaling their soul.*' She shuddered. 'Not only stops you returning to the collective conscious. It leaves nothing of you to return in another form. You're gone, like that!' she clapped her hands an inch from Will's nose.

'Okay. So we kill it.'

'We can try, but there are two big problems. One.' She gestured at their wasted bodies. 'Cats are fast, and we really aren't. And two?' She measured off two fingers. 'The cats are only the avatar that a Chordewa sends out to feed, while it sleeps. Meaning it's probably somewhere in this building, somewhere guarded by its magic. So if we catch the cat, it says here the Chordewa is doomed to sleep until it fades to nothing.'

'Wouldn't we still be better off killing the little bastard?'

'I don't think we can.' She covered Will's hand with her own. 'It can't leave when the exits are locked. And why would it? For a demon who preys on the dying this place is fucking perfect.'

'Regular smorgasbord,' Will said. 'Why don't we tell someone? Father George will be in at the weekend and...'

'Ha! If you hadn't seen what you've seen, would you be listening to me right now? Plus that's three days away. Can we afford to wait that long?'

'Point taken.'

'So we find the cat and we trap it.'

Will sighed, leaning his head back to stare up at the cream-coloured ceiling blinds shielding them from sun. He said nothing for a few moments.

Birdsong came muffled on a waft of garden-scented wind; the softness mixing with harsher clouds of spray polish, and the staccato crackles of Mrs C's plastic apron. Even Robbie made no noises louder than the scrunching of peanut shells.

Molly looked up to see what fascinated Will. There was nothing there but a few dead flies. Trapped between canvas and glass, their grotesque outlines were of bodies and wings, with their legs folded neatly inwards, like tiny cadavers laid out on a vast hammock; struck down without warning. *Or perhaps*, she thought, *I just see that because I'm here.*

'I'm with you so far as it goes but I can't do much.' Will gestured a bony hand down the length of his torso and legs, emaciated beneath their blanket-wrap. 'I can't sit up on my own, never mind chase supernatural cats. I'm really good at lying around the place, if that counts.' He glanced back toward the corridor, and leaned as close as he was able, lowering his voice to a mere zephyr. 'That's basically all you need from bait.'

Sound ceased for that moment, not even the swish of Mrs C's apron, as Molly digested that snippet. 'I don't know. That could be the most dangerous part.'

'Oh. Yeah. And I've got such a lot to lose? Come on, Mol. You brought all this up. We have to give it at least one try.'

She looked around her. As always the room was deserted, with no one to watch over their plotting but a potty-mouthed parrot. 'Okay. Tonight then. Just don't take any of their bloody knockout pills. You need to be awake!'

*

Molly came slowly into consciousness, aware it was late. She raised the bed to slide off more easily and grabbed crutches in favour of the wheelchair. The night-time lull had already set in. A few TVs played softly in various rooms; low conversation drifted from the staff room behind Reception; Robbie muttered to himself in the darkened conservatory.

The hallway's bluish night-lighting was split by the work of one small table lamp and the flickering TV-glow dancing lazily from Will's open door.

Chomi was on his chest, her head stretched forward to lap delicately at Will's pale, dry lips, her dark tongue dipping in and out of a smoky-blue haze flowing steadily from his mouth to hers.

Molly lifted a crutch and hurled it, javelin-style. Accurate, from a hundred stick-heaving contests, the rubber ferule caught the beast on its head and knocked it over the far edge. She felt rather than heard the thud and clatter of the crutch hitting the wall. She lurched forward, yelling for Beth, competing with the monitor now screeching from the bedside.

She fell toward him, intending to check vital signs. Will was pale, his eyes squeezed tightly shut against the world and then flickered open. Molly felt a slight relief.

Then she was gently, firmly, removed, and someone was handing her the spent crutch-missile. She caught a momentary glimpse of a black shape, flowing around the corner of the door and out of sight at speed.

'Chomi,' Molly said. 'The cat. It was on the bed.'

'A cat? Is that all? Well don't worry about it now. We'll deal with it.' She was an agency nurse, not one of usual night staff and unaware, she turned her back on Molly, and hurried back to help Beth in attending Will.

The electronic screech was staunched abruptly and Molly hurried to peer around the door. She could see the signs on the screen were thankfully stable and moving with a regular rhythm. Low voices, calm tones. She glanced along the passage in both directions. She knew the animal would still be in here ... somewhere. She began a fresh search, starting at the reception desk and working her way along every room with an open door. Nothing she had seen so far led her to believe her adversary walked through closed doors or walls.

From the darkened end room the squawk and mutter of a sleepy parrot drifted into her thoughts. She lurched through the doors, flicked one set of lights on and searched under every chair and table. As with all the other rooms there was nothing out of the norm. Chomi had vanished.

Molly didn't want to sleep. Nor did she want to listen to the hushed tones of nursing staff keeping her friend alive just metres from her own bed. She had told Will about the Chordewa and he had insisted on being the tethered goat, leaving his door open to invite it in. He had argued that his condition made him a prime candidate, and he'd obviously been right. She should never have let him. And then to fall asleep, to leave him vulnerable, that was unforgivable. She picked up the TV remote and flopped into an arm chair.

Molly didn't want to sleep. The cat had found her once and its wheedling, insidious mesmer scared her more than she could say. The websites she had spent hours Googling had told her little beyond how the demon seeks out the sick and dying. It had come to her first, before the cancer-raddled Will. Did that mean she was closer to her end than she had been told?

Molly didn't want to sleep.

*

'Bastard. Fetch the cart. Bastard. Shut up Robbie. Fetch the cart.'

Molly woke with a pounding headache and pressure in her left arm. Prising her lids open was an effort. So much harder than usual, though she knew for sure she had not succumbed to the little red sleeping pills Beth was constantly trying to push at her.

'Bastard. Fuck off. Fetch the cart.'

She rolled her head toward the indistinct flurry of red and blue. Robbie was bobbing and weaving his scarlet head, clipped and impotent azure wings flapping madly. He was rattling the entire cage. Unable to fly or run he sidled back and fore, raising first one foot, high and to the side, and then the other, like some exaggerated parody of dance, and all the while screeching his abusive mimicry. Something had him agitated beyond his usual state of squawk and blasphemy.

She turned her head toward a lower, deeper sound, and was face to face with Chomi.

'Shit!' She leapt to her feet. 'Fuck!'

The cat didn't move beyond a slow blink of its bronze eyes.

Molly grabbed one of her sticks from beside the chair and swiped. Chomi skittered across the tiles, scrabbling for purchase on the cold and shiny surface and once still, crouched, hissing and clicking her anger to the room in general, seemingly confused and disorientated, as cats seldom were. She realised her options were about as limited as Robbie's repertoire. Chomi always dealt with whatever came her way in the cat fashion of total disdain, but an angry Chomi, one intent on doing harm, was new; and, she felt, potentially lethal. Hurting any animal went against everything Molly stood for; but was this a cat at all?

Whatever it was, it wailed pure displeasure, lashing its thin black tail from tip to base one moment, and the next it launched straight toward Molly. She dodged it, thrashing her stick from side to side, missing her target as wholly and completely as Chomi did not. Scythe-like claws raked across her face and chest, neat and clinical yet inflicting no pain.

The cat bounced onto the cage top with back arched and fur ruffled into fuzzy haloes. She clawed through the bars at Robbie, who pounded at her with his wings, sending a shower of seed and grit and small feathers raining to the floor. 'Fetch the cart. Bastard cart. Fetch the bastard.' He flapped at the paws sliding between the bars and bobbed frantically. 'Fuck cart off. Robbie. Robbie. Hello. Hello.'

In another time Molly might have smiled at the mixed phrases born of Robbie's panic, but his frenzy was too close to her own. She looked down the corridor and saw Beth walk across to Reception with only a brief glance in the direction of the sudden noise. People were used to the bird squawking. It did not warrant her attention.

Molly spun back just in time to deflect a fresh attack. She hoped she'd got in a hit when the animal flashed past her, a long, furry streak of anger. It landed close to the door, sliding through it, gaining traction, and headed toward the exit. Molly followed and yelled at Beth to: 'Stop it!'

Half way along the stretch, the door to the cleaner's store stood open by a few inches and Chomi veered into it. Molly pumped her legs a little faster, still screaming at Beth to, 'Catch that bloody cat.' If she could only shut the creature in. She held both hands out, ready to slam the door. A few more paces and the door flipped open as though kicked by some unseen mule. A white barrier, blocking her view of both desk and nursing staff. Molly halted, resting a hand against the wall to steady her momentum.

Calmly, with no hint of concern, Mrs C stepped from the store room. An M&S raincoat was draped over her left arm, a voluminous shopping bag dangled from her right hand, as anonymous as anyone, on any street, anywhere. She fixed Molly with coppery eyes, as dark and shaded as the fresh bruises deepening on her forehead and bare right arm. She said nothing, only smiled, bowed politely and gestured toward the Residents' Lounge.

Molly looked back along her gaze and saw a head showing above the chair back; saw the shadow of legs beneath it and the crutches laid alongside on the floor.

She saw herself. Molly glanced down at sturdy legs unsupported by stick or wheel for the first time in months.

Mrs C drew her hand down the side of Molly's face. The touch was ephemeral as though she were not there; except that she *was*. The woman closed the cupboard door, very softly, and strolled toward the front exit. She was calling out some mumbled thing to Beth and then paused to smile back at Molly one final time before she drifted into the night.

Molly barely noticed the crash cart plough through her.

# Old Hat

It's an old hat – that's just old hat.
On crumpled black velvet
dust gathers without care.
Bought on a whim
and we laughed, we pair.
Wear it and smile
just to feel, to dare,
A red rose holds back the brim,
creased beyond repair.

# Winter Eve

'WHAT ARE YOU doing.' Nain's questions were seldom queries. Mostly they were direct orders to cease and desist all actions.

Tegan tried not to look overly pissed off at those opening salvos of interrogation and went onto a counter attack with a question-statement of her own. 'I'm sewing a button. What does it look like.'

'Don't be cheeky, my girl. Young ladies don't say things like that. And they don't back chat their elders neither.'

Mouthing along with her grandmother's rote put down, Tegan bent over her coat and nibbled off the thread.

'I saw that,' Nain added. 'You'll cut your tongue off and the Old Nick'll get in. You just see.'

Tegan sighed and willed herself not to ask what that was supposed to mean. Tonight was not the night for drawing flack and it was a futile exercise in any case. Nain's sayings and superstitions were as abstruse as they were numerous. Family rumour was she made half of them up as she went along but it was never wise to challenge her on them. Most of her repertoire seemed to involve death, or demons, or both, and the old girl got quite excitable if anyone questioned their veracity. Or worse still defied the various riders attached. Never put shoes on a table or there will be a death in the family; always hide the cutlery in thunder storms or you will get struck down through the window, butter a cat's paws when you move into a new home or it will go wandering off and take the good fortune with it. The old lady had thousands of them, and Tegan was fairly sure she'd heard them all since Nain had come to live with them.

The local TV news had just begun, reminding Tegan she was running very late. She flung the mended coat over her shoulders and headed for the door. 'Yes Nain. I'll be careful. Sorry, I've got to go. I promised Lauren I'd meet her in half an hour.'

'Going out? This time of night? On Nos Calan Gaeaf? Don't, Teggy. Please don't.'

The old woman reached out a skinny arm to her only granddaughter and Tegan was touched to see a genuine anxiety her grandmother's lined face. *The old dear really does worry*, she thought. 'It's just a bit of fun Nain. No one really thinks they're going to meet the devil out there. Too crowded for one thing.'

'It's not him I'm worried on, annwyl. I heard the ponies out past the twmp. Calling they were, like Ceffyl-dwr. It's not safe. Not tonight.'

'Yes it is Nain. Don't worry about me. I'll see you in the morning.' Tegan hurried back to drop a kiss on Nain's white curls and then made a dash for the outside world, where the 21st century held sway.

Only one stop but she was still running late by the time her train pulled into Ponty station, and she jogged the ten-minute-walk to the 'Feathers'. 'Thank God for txt,' she muttered, and sprinted across the Broadway, raising the traditional salute at beeps from rush hour tailenders.

In dark and damp streets the last noisy gaggles of trick-or-treaters were woo-wooing past her in cheap rubbery masks or witchy hats, or both. Most escorted by harassed parents on their way home as evening drew on. Clumps of teens in half-arsed get-ups had lost interest and hung about swigging cider and jeering at anyone that caught their unsteady gaze.

Tegan was glad she had left her 'disguise' in her bag as she strode out past another of these rag-tag herds. Nain's caustic comments seemed to hold a bit more substance than when she'd stood in the kitchen holding the torn-sheet ghost outfit between finger and thumb and said, 'Not put much effort in have you.'

'Well at least I don't have to worry about make-up and stuff,' Tegan had argued. 'It's irony, see.'

Seeing identical outfits amongst those urchins Tegan had to acknowledge that an old sheet with holes in might well be simple but it was never ever going to be a class act. 'Dammed lazy if you ask me,' Mam had said. 'I could do you a good pirate. Or a Dracula. That'd be nice. Bit of red lippy down your chin. Lovely.'

Tegan's thoughts on that whole conversation were not for family consumption. Dracula? Where was the imagination in that? No. At least the sheet-ghost could be explained away as kitsch. And more importantly? It was discardable in a hurry. Mam and Nain would go nuts if they knew.

There were ponies out tonight and she found that odd. The wild ponies seldom came in off the hills so close to the town. Perhaps they knew? Maybe the glut of apples and sweet treats and maybe the possibility of polo

-mints attracted them more than any other night? Perhaps they knew that when the veil was thinner human kind had better things to do than chase a few mud spattered ponies? She paused, watching a trio of them a little distance off, cropping grass, raising their heads now and then to keep an eye on passers-by or keep a wary watch toward distant fireworks from some early Guy Fawkes party.

Tegan called quietly. The largest of the three mares looked toward her, ears pricked. Even from this distance Tegan could hear her scenting the air, snuffling and huffing, her neck stretched out in a vague challenge, ears back and teeth showing pale in a dark-brown face. 'Shush, there now, girl, nothing to worry about.' Tegan edged slowly forward to within a few feet of the mare, her hand out. Three more paces and she could touch the wild animal's forehead blaze.

The mare stared at her for a moment and shuffled a few steps to one side, ears forward now, scenting the air and whickering quietly, considering whether this person posed a threat. She stretched her neck out once again brushing her velvet nose against Tegan's arm before shaking her mane and putting in a few casual paces from this odd-smelling human before returning to her browsing.

Tegan smiled and hurried on.

The *Feathers* was close now and she came across a very different style of treater thronging the main bar. Students in horror disguises straight out of the hire shops and drama school's props cupboards. Most had fallen back on the usual Witches, Skeletons, Satans and Zombies and only a few of the more dedicated aficionados were splendid in handmade extravaganzas. Two Jack the Rippers, several pirates and three Faery Queens; one of them male, the image of that snow queen with goatee beard and welly-boots would stay with her for a long while. Among the Uni revellers lurked the Pagan crowd, loitering in their blacks and purples and deepest reds and greens, waiting for their Samhain ceremonies around the Rocking Stone, out across the common.

Tegan stood tall and peered across the melee for her friend. There, near the far doors she spotted Lauren's mass of deepest black hair streaked with a crimson sheen. It was hard to miss even amongst present company. She got a round from the bar and squeezed through the crowd to plonk herself on the bench seat next to her friend.

'What time is this?' Lauren asked.

'Don't. I've had enough of that tonight off the Nain.' She took a long swill from the pint Lauren had already got her in, savouring the slightly bitter tang soothing her dry throat as it flowed. It was flat after sitting there so long, but it hit the spot. She nodded at the crowds. 'Got anything special marked out?'

'Not really.'

Tegan stared around the packed bar with a snort of exasperation. 'Oh yeah. I see your problem. God forbid we'd be spoiled for choice.'

'There's plenty of people. Just none of them stand out— No-one special.'

Tegan nodded, took another slurp at her Guinness, and shuddered. Once the whistle was wetted – it was just flat beer. 'Maybe over at the Stones?' she said.

'No. Far too crowded.'

'That's bit of a contradiction.'

'Not really.' Lauren was watching the crowd and frowning. 'Maybe we should have stuck with the Wyvern Arms. Much better area, and the river goes right past it.'

'Can if you like. We've still got time.'

Considering the idea and dismissing it in three seconds flat, Lauren went back to her close scrutiny of the crowd. 'This'll do. There's enough here to choose from.'

They sat in near silence, drinking drinks and watching as the crowd thinned. Students soon drifted away to the parties that would be blasting into the wee hours, and not long before closing time the Druids filed out in an ordered unofficial procession toward the Rocking Stone. *They're always that way*, Tegan thought. *Tidy like.*

The Wiccans followed on in quiet groups, just as dignified if a little less militant. The mass exodus left the bar curiously subdued, with just the pub regulars and a handful of furtive Goths propping up various sections of bar or table.

Lauren was taking notice all of a sudden. Nursing her pint and relaxing against the bench seat's high wooden back, watching the remaining drinkers with narrowed, predatory eyes.

Tegan sat back in the bench and waited. This was Lauren's gig, she merely the eager acolyte. The old wood planks behind her head felt solid, comforting in their oaken placidity. Old pews from the Llanwirth Road Chapel, she'd been told, imbued with a century of prayer and self-denial. A century of heads had rubbed the patina into these boards as they listened to a weekly diet of hellfire and brimstone, whilst contemplating the roast lamb for their Sunday dinner baking slowly inside polished black-iron ranges. That predictability and tradition was soothing.

She wasn't going to wallow in daydreams just now, when Lauren was on the move. Pouring the last half pint down her throat Tegan scuttled to catch her up.

Away from the pub's soft yellow light, the common was goth-black and she was hard put to keep up with her friend. Ahead of them a torch light wavered across the common, with the noise from two pairs of feet being guided along its beam. They followed at a small distance, making sure these two were not just walking to their car.

There was a tang of wood smoke and spent gunpowder in the air from the nearby bonfire mixing with the more pungent scents of wet earth and damp bracken. Tegan could hear the ponies calling a way off to the left, and a faint rush of water to her right. Ahead of them the drink-laden laddos stumbled and cussed their way across rough ground toward the Broadway.

She looked toward Lauren for a signal but her friend was already off into the shadows. This was it. Her limbs tingled and her mind had begun to lose focus, light-headed with the onset. All the talking and planning was culminating in twin anticipation of relish and dread. But Tegan knew this had to be.

She was hyperventilating. That anticipation was a drug. The nerves and doubts she had begun the evening with were washed away. She flicked her long hair back from her eyes and broke into a run, stretching her limbs out into full strength. The bumps and dips of rough grass no longer trip hazards, the dark lessening with moonlight slicing through a gap in the clouds.

The ponies that she had seen earlier were scattering before her, kicking up their heels with tails and heads high, calling shrilly to one another, yet not through fright. They called in greeting and curiosity.

She ran after them for a few yards, almost forgetting herself, and Lauren, in the *moment*. She stumbled as her friend and mentor pushed her back on course.

Two figures were running before them. Tripping and cursing and scattering chunks of their costumes in an effort to run unencumbered.

Lauren and Tegan ran on behind.

Following. No. They were hunting. Racing back and fore behind the prey, pushing them toward the river. This was Tegan's first. This was what Lauren had told her of and what she had changed her into. Bitten and re-animated. And so alive.

Across the road and onto the bank. Just a short distance from the Broadway, with street lights and traffic spreading across to pick out highlights of the scene.

Even on a dark night the water foamed and roared. White water sluicing between far banks. Not deep most people thought. Not with all the rocks causing the water to boil as it did in churning, roiling threads. Just the current that was dangerous. No one swam here.

She could see their quarry in the light of passing cars, teetering on the bank's muddy brink, their faces paler than the water beyond them. Both were overly black-haired and black-clad in a cute if tragic-emo kind of way. Tonight their appeal was more basic than mere fashion.

Lauren reared up, slashing at the pair, shaking her

snaggle-toothed head, mane thrashing, tail lashing, she snatched the taller of the two in her river-ward leap. Tegan heard his scream cut off when the waters closed over him.

Tegan reared up and lunged. She heard her own meal scream. Just once. Before she took him below.

# Haiku

## Bees
A shimmer of bees.
Lavender scented breakfast
There for the harvest.

## On the Radio
Radio writers,
chattering all through the night.
Make so little sense.

## Bats
Little flittermouse,
Dropping from the eaves at dusk
To hunt blood suckers

# Jack Jumps Out of the Box

THAT HEART-SHAPED, heart-breaking face had enough make-up to keep Broadway floating for half a season. She was dressed in black, from her sailor-cut shirt right down to her Oxford-bags and pixie boots. She'd traded in those signature gold curls for choppy black spikes. She was a different girl. But not different enough. I'd recognise that chassis anywhere.

She was staring out into the street where the clouds still promised to rain on everyone's parade. I crossed the room and slid up behind her. Close enough for the point of my .38 Special to get friendly with her ribs. 'Hi there Goldie,' I said.

She didn't turn around. She kept right on eyeballing the people drifting in and out of the main gate. I guess that's how she knew I was coming.

'Hey, D'Ranyer,' she whispered. 'You took your time. And it's Jill. No one's called me Goldie in years.'

She was a cool one. 'Anyone still call you Bo-Peep?' I said. 'Or Muffet? You've got through one hell of a lot of names, kid.'

'Yeah. You know how it is. New mark – new moniker.'

She was trying hard to stay calm. Then she turned on me with those big baby-blues. They were brimming tears and I knew right then I was onto a loser. She'd got me that way before and I'd told myself I wasn't gonna fall for it. But her eyes were so red and swollen you'd've thought someone had pasted extra lips around her eyeballs. I looked her up and down. She may have gotten tired and rumpled but she looked good. 'You still got it Goldie.'

She shrugged. Those gelled-up spikes of hair rustled with every shake of her head.

'Where's Jack?' I asked her.

'He's dying.'

I wasn't counting on that. It's not something we come across so much back in the Tales. I stood back for a better look. 'All the more reason he should come back now.' I said. 'Over the border he'll be safe.'

'Not without clearing his name. All a legend has is his legend. Once that's gone?' She slumped against the wall, her chin pressed into her chest like a half-deflated balloon.

The dame had it right. Sometimes all a man's got is his name. 'Ma says it's a bum deal, and she'll guarantee you get a fair hearing,' I said.

Goldie wasn't buying. 'I ain't stupid, D'Ranyer. It's not Ma's call. And I'm not getting nowhere near Tales 'til I can prove we're in the clear.'

'Then take me to Jack. Let's hear what the man has to say.'

She shrugged. 'I'll take ya. But I gotta warn you. He ain't saying much of anything right now.' She led the way down corridors that were pale grey like old porridge. Dimly lit and stinking of old floor mops and piss. Then we were standing outside the ICU peering through the glass door panel at Jack, unconscious with tubes and cables all over. 'Yeah. He's not so talkative,' I said to her. 'So if you don't want those goons coming back to persuade you? You'd better spill. Who wants Jack taken out?' I asked.

'What if I say I had no idea?'

'I'd say you're lying.'

'And you'd be wrong. I have no idea. Believe me. I sure as hell got no idea who jumped us.' She shook her head, sending out another whispering rattle, like the shake of a small and stealthy porcupine tail. 'Can't think who. Folks really like Jack. ''Cepting the Giants' crew. Payback on the Beanstalk fiasco, maybe? Jack was working for the Palace. That's all I know.'

Her logic made sense. Except no Giant 's ever set foot in the Palace. This was an inside job. 'Jack was in the palace that day because he got a call?' I said. 'Someone there put out the APB on you guys.'

'The Queen,' said Goldie. 'She's passed judgement.'

'Off with your heads?'

A door slammed way down the corridor and we both caught a glimpse of two half-ogres checking out room by room, and getting closer. I pushed her into the ICU to collect Jack, and we were back on Ma's estate before you could name a certain gold-spinning dwarf.

*

I took a ride over to the Palace soon as we got back. I still had to find out why Jack got the full force of Palace justice on his case.

Inside was pretty quiet which had me spooked. Over a thousand people worked that joint. You'd think you'd run across some of them once in a while.

I wasn't sure if I was looking for the King, the Queen,

or their boy, that folks called the Knave. A bad seed. Not many had seen him since he burned down the great hall and left home under a cloud of smoke and bad vibes. I'd prowled around for a half hour before I found the King, Reginald Albert King, and his lady Queen. They were getting cosy around a fire and drinking tea.

I was half way across the room and never saw the meatheads until they had the drop on me. Those .45 cannons looked like peashooters in those fists. I didn't want to give any excuse to try them out so I let them manhandle me over to the fireplace. I was going that way anyhow.

The Queen snapped her fingers and her goons shoved me down on my knees. 'D'Ranyer,' she was smiling fit to burn. 'How good of you to call.'

She could turn on the charm, if you could just get past those dead eyes. It was like staring a gator straight down its cold-blooded mean-ass schnozzle.

'And what brings you here?' the King said. 'Still schlepping for that Goose woman?'

'It's an honest buck,' I said. 'Most times.'

The King sat back, tapping his fingers on the arm of his chair. 'I hear she's harbouring wanted fugitives,' He said.

'I wouldn't know. I've been out of town.'

'We heard.' Queenie added. 'Now I'm asking why you're in my palace.'

'Would you believe the two dime tour?' Those goons might look dumb but they knew their trade. Knew exactly how much a skull could take before it splits like a green cantaloupe. Just enough to have little tweeting birds and stars circling around my skull but not quite enough to send me to la la land. I blinked and waited for the room to stop jiving around before I looked the old dame right back in the eye. You gotta show them you won't be intimidated. Killed maybe. But not intimidated.

'What was that fox-boy?' she purred. 'Speak up.'

'Oh hell. Make that the dollar de-luxe tour. I always like the scenic route.'

One goon hauled me up while his pal planted a fist in my ribs, my face, my ribs. Once, twice, maybe three times. Can't say for sure. After a while you lose count. They were pros. They worked me over pretty good. Never once did I black out. They didn't want me to miss a thing.

'Still not saying?' The Queen stood beside me. I didn't bow. She tipped my head with her foot to look me in the eyes. 'Tell Ma she needs to try harder. And you? I can double whatever she's paying.'

'Double of nothing is zip,' I said.

My face hit the floor as she stomped back to her seat. 'You talk to him, Reggie.' She was getting snippy.

'Sit,' he said. I got hauled up and folded into a chair. A glass of brandy got shoved into my paw. I took a mouthful, waited for the sting to race around every cut gum and cracked lip, before I swallowed. It was good liquor. Sipping grade. I downed the rest in one and held out for a refill.

Reggie nodded and I was poured another half glass.

'What do you want, D'Ranyer?' he said. 'Why're you here?'

'I'm helping out an old friend. That's it.' I sipped a little more brandy, careful this time, trying not to get it tainted by my bleeding lips.

'Ah. The girl.' He nodded. 'Nice, but not what a parent wants for their boy.'

That was a new one on me. I knew Goldie had ambition, but the Knave? I took another slug from the glass while I thought. Fast. 'Didn't know she'd ever met him.' I said. 'You tell me what's going on. I'll think about it.' I wasn't about to sell out, but stalling was preferable to having the twins work me over again. I'd seen what they did to Jack.

'Our son has been a little wayward.' The King sighed, deep and heavy. He was just a father trying to straighten out his kid. I didn't feel sorry for him.

'Kid's get that way,' I murmured, still stalling.

'He runs around with all kinds. Upsetting neighbouring kingdoms right and left. It's no secret he turned out wild. We see him perhaps twice a year, if that. Fine while he was still a kid. But he's a man now. He has duties. He needs to marry the right girl. Point blank refused the deal we had lined up. Bottom line? Her father called us out and we're on the brink of war. All down to that stupid boy.'

'I know the royal marriage thing is a big deal but I didn't see how Jack's involved. All he did was work a few favours.'

'All?' Queenies voice rose an octave. 'Our son insulted her in front of the court. Called her...' She stopped, red in the face. Redder than me. 'You tell him, Reggie' she snapped.

Reggie raised an eyebrow and glanced my way. For a moment we almost understood each other. Then duty got him back on track. 'Tart.' He said. 'My son called the Princess of Glaslookin a tart.'

I wanted to say he had a point. The Princess was no princess. Everyone knew she was a party girl. She used to be Snow White. But then she got shovelled up in a snow blower and spread all over town. Snow was her thing. Most of it went up that dainty little nose. I sloshed another mouthful of liquid courage and set the glass down. 'Out of my league. I don't do world politics. Begging your pardon.'

'But we have to get him back. We have to make him apologise.'

'So you want me to find your boy as well as Jack? I don't even know what he looks like.'

'Oh,' said Queenie, 'I think you do.'

*

I got back to the farm late. Security was on high at Ma's compound. A half dozen meatheads from the Old Shoe gang were on point and getting past them was tough.

Inside was no better. I've never seen the place so stirred up. Not even after Ma's old man got fingered for throwing some guy down some stairs.

Jack was sitting by the fountain in the courtyard when I finally got to him, slumped in a chair like a month old bread poultice, pale and wrinkled and covered in patches of blue and green. Except you can wipe off the mould. Those bruises were going to take a deal more healing. 'Jack.' I nodded slowly.

'D'Ranyer. I thought you'd be here sooner.'

He was grinning ear to ear.

I rubbed at my puffed up face. 'You about to tell me what I got this for?' I said. 'Or are we waiting for the re-runs?'

That shrug, another grin.

I thought I knew this guy. Seems me and most of the world had it wrong.

'Does the King need a reason?' I asked.

'Usually. Might not be one we'd think about.'

Suddenly the light snapped on. He was that guy. The Knave of Hearts, aka Jack of Hearts. But he was our Jack. And our Jack never could stop himself playing the dumb ass hero.

'The way I see it?' he said. 'Someone dissed out on the Queen's tarts.'

# You and Me, Pop:
# Whist and the Bird Tattoo

Just 90 years young or you would have been, Pop,
had the fates been kinder to people you knew.
Did you ever recalled the good times.
When TV blared in the family room, but,
Sing Something Simple and you and me, Pop,
playing whist on those long winter nights.
Me and you, as the kettle rattled on the Aga hob.
Long walks, and leaning on the gate, where you
    counted sheep,
pointing your gnarled crook, as they cropped,
with heads down and feet stamping,
and the dog, in frustration, herded ducks on the river.
He never caught but one.

That hay dust wheeze, even after the farm,
and your little blue pills beneath your tongue.
The laughter we shared, between you and me, Pop,
and that faded bird tattoo, is how I recall you most.
A present from Rome, your spoils of war.
Not a heron, you said, nor our Clan's Tercel might.
It was lost in translation and the Grahams were
    tamed.
Falcon was bluebird, ever searching white cliffs.
Our spiked rose to red sun topping pale lotus bloom,
more fitting your gentleness, in so many ways,

that I often wondered.
Did it become you, Pop? Or you all the while?

The jokes you played on your Welsh maid, Anice,
King of wind-up, all po faced and serious
as you fed her line by teasing line.
You never fooled me, Pop. Those twinkles in your eye,
    a sure sign every time.
Top brick off the chimney, Mother always moaned.
    But she never understood us, nor ever tried, I
    suppose.
You and me, Pop, you and me, separated by wounded
    pride not our own
that festered into feud and fugue to be fed by fear.
And we lost it all, you and me, Pop. Too late to make
    amends.

But Happy Birthday nevertheless, maybe the Downs
    remember – You and me, Pop.
With our whist, and the bird tattoo.

# A Taste of Culture

HE WAS HUNGRY. But the first stand, crudely painted in garish colours, proclaimed its contents to be 'Earth Friendly.' He averted his eyes. This was England. Roasting oxen and warmed bread – that's how it had been at English country fayres in years past. Now it was all lentils and tofu and other vegetarian creeds that offended him deeply.

He shrugged lightly and moved around the gathering's perimeter to gauge the extent of delicacies on offer. Darkness had only just fallen and he was in no hurry – happy to feel, if not part of the crowd, then at least in contact with life; not merely humanity, but life itself: and the music that rose all around him, so vibrant, so invasive with its rapid, heartbeat rhythm. It pleased him greatly. These modern sounds were unfamiliar to him, but then every generation renewed the angst of misunderstood youth through its Art. It was part of the mystique of life.

He moved on, admiring the scenes before him. People, and so many of them in such a small place, and so varied. His stomach muttered discontent, reminding him he had to fill the void before he could think of doing anything else. What would a fayre have to offer other than sweetmeats doled out for infants and would-be infants alike?

He could see any number of options. Chinese? No. He had never found them satisfying. Italian? Maybe not. Even the smell of garlic gave him indigestion. A tall black woman brushed passed him, her cinnamon scent lingering with him as she walked away. He paused, rotating slowly to follow her progress, until she vanished into the crowd. He'd follow if she were alone – the bulky lad trailing behind her could be a stranger, but somehow he doubted it.

The lights on a ride close by him so stung his eyes with their flaring intensity that he had to raise a hand to block the worst of the glare. Maybe he was getting too old for all this frivolity. Perhaps he would skip all this noise and settle for a liquid supper, like in the old days when life was so much simpler. There was an inn on the far side of the green. Quiet in comparison to this mêlée, but suitable. He'd find something there. But a companion? He never drank alone. It was not civilised.

He cast around for an easier option, and almost blundered into a burger-stand. He shuddered at an abomination surpassing tinned spaghetti and, reeling away from the hideous stench, quite literally stumbled into a small, lone figure huddled in the shelter of the vehicle, borrowing warmth from the occupant's vile trade. Engrossed in the contents of her purse, the young woman was unaware of his presence until she looked up, face flushed under the fairground lights. She was an open invitation. Wide deep green eyes, and soft flawless skin made more tempting with its painted-on beauty. And a neck that arched in slender elegance as she looked up into his own dark eyes.

'Oh! Pardon Monsieur.' Her voice was low, but oddly

childlike in her surprise at his sudden appearance.

He bowed low, and smiled, anticipating a treat he hadn't thought to find in Britain's rural wilderness. It didn't matter where on this earth he found himself, it would always be hard to beat a good French red.

# Afterword

IT WOULD BE nice to say these stories were inspired by great events or that I have a message to relay to the world at large, but truth be told most of the stories included here come almost by accident and are largely plundered from my store of folktales, myths and legends. I love to write, and always have, and I am always happiest putting a new face on those ancient tales.

'A Taste of Culture', a very short story written for the *Mammoth Book of Dracula* edited by Stephen Jones. I was never more surprised than when it was accepted because I had written for fun and never remotely expected it to be accepted. It just goes to show, you never can tell what will tickle an editor's fancy. First published in 1997, the volume has been translated into several languages, and reprinted several times on both sides of the Atlantic, so it was a gag worth the writing.

'Damnation Seize My Soul' was commissioned for the Newcon anthology *Dark Currents*. It was intended to be a straight pirate tale, but somehow got tangled up with the universal hero being washed through the eons on the twin currents of revenge and justice.

'Drawing Down the Moon' was commissioned by Dean Drinkel for Western Legends Publishing. It appeared in the *Grimorium Verum,* volume three of *Tres Liborum Prohibitorum*. My pieces for volumes one and two can be found in my first collection, *Leinster Gardens and Other Subtleties*. For volume three I was asked for a tale that might suit a witch's grimoire. But, being a practicing witch, I was eager not to use the clichéd evil harridan as my lead role, yet wanted to give her an edge of menace and power. So what better than a Witch of Thessaly running a greasy spoon on the Isle of Dogs exacting her revenge.

'Gallery Green', published in *Terror Scribes,* is about obsessions, and what appears to be an artist's fixation with his one creation.

'Green Tea', published in *Salvo 8,* arose from an acquaintance banging on about the medicinal benefits of elderberries, but like many things these little fruits do contain toxic substances; in minute quantities it is true. I had fun wondering whether elderberry poisoning could be achieved.

'Grey Magic for Lovers' appeared in the BFS publication *New Horizons* and was inspired by the question posed at a writing group about the term 'magic realism'. Impish perversity inspired me to write about the dangerous consequences of real magic – should it exist!

'Jack, Out of the Box' was written for a Grimm's Tales anthology, *Father Grim's Story Book*, though it is more mother goose in real terms when a noir, gum-shoe detective goes in search of the missing hero, Jack. I love noir fiction and this seemed an ideal vehicle. The image of my vulpine detective standing in the shadows in mac and fedora was irresistible.

'Mayday Comes Askew' is another gag, written for the Pagan magazine *Tales of the Greenmantle*. It asks what would the old pagan deities have done when Oliver Cromwell banned all of the old holidays such as Beltane and Yule.

'Midnight Twilight' was also commissioned, this time for the volume *Alt-Zombie*. Not being a huge reader of zombie tales I played a little fast and loose with that one, set in the land of the midnight sun, combining it with Scandinavian myths and 19th century literature.

'Princess Born' is another comic tale, this time written for *Grim and Grimmer Volume 1*, a small anthology of reinvented fairy tales – and I shall leave the reader to decide who or what my inspirations may have been!

'The Abused and Him' is the earliest piece in this collection, appearing in *Visionary Tongue* way back in 1996. Perhaps an odd choice to include here, but is an early publication and important because of that. It began life as a nightmare related to me by a friend, which proves the old adage 'never tell a writer anything – it may end up in a book'.

'Thirteenth Day', from *Estronomicon*, stays with the

theme of pagan legends and combined the notion of the Wild Hunt with the unending circle of seasons played out between Holly and Oak Kings, with the added prompt of an old (possibly pagan) Scottish carol that gave rise to 'Twelve Days of Christmas'. Inspiration from many sources there!

'Winter Eve' is a classic Halloween tale, which appeared in *Ethereal Tales 9*, and takes the Welsh tradition of *Nos Calan Gaeaf* and the myths of horse spirits that abound around then. I loved the notion of a rites of passage pushing through into the other world when the veil is at its thinnest.

Though this volume is primarily short fiction I thought long and hard and eventually decided to include poetry. I have never really seen myself as a poet. Leaving aside the Haiku, which I penned purely for fun, the few poems I have written found a place in a variety of publications. *City Canal* and *Corinna's Reply* both arose from studying for my BA in English Literature.

So there we have it: my *Fables and Fabrications*. I had a blast writing them and really hope you have as much fun in the reading.

Jan Edwards, 2016

## Also from The Penkhull Press

*Sussex Tales* – Jan Edwards
*Tangerine Monday Blues* – Jan Edwards
*Winter Downs* – Jan Edwards
*House of Shadows* – Misha Herwin
*Picking Up the Pieces* – Misha Herwin
*It Never Was Worthwhile* –Jem Shaw and Malcolm
     Havard
*The Larks* – Jem Shaw

## Penkhull Slims

*Fables and Fabrications* – Jan Edwards
*It's the End of the World* – Nic Hale

Made in the USA
Charleston, SC
12 May 2016